Norman Hunter was born in 1899 in Sydenham, London. After leaving school he worked as an advertising copywriter, and also made over two hundred appearances on stage as a conjuror at Maskelyne and Devant's famous magic theatre. His first Professor Branestawn book was published in 1933, and a sequel followed in 1937. After living in South Africa for over twenty years, he returned to England in 1969 and wrote a further ten Professor Branestawn books, the last of which appeared in 1983. He died in 1995.

Also available by Norman Hunter:

The Incredible Adventures of Professor Branestawm
The Peculiar Triumph of Professor Branestawm
Professor Branestawm Stories

The Dribblesome Teapots

and Other Incredible Stories

NORMAN HUNTER

WITH ILLUSTRATIONS BY FRITZ WEGNER

RED FOX CLASSICS

THE DRIBBLESOME TEAPOTS
AND OTHER INCREDIBLE STORIES

A Red Fox Classics Book 978 1 849 41925 3

This edition published in Great Britain by Red Fox Classics,
an imprint of Random House Children's Publishers UK
A Random House Group Company

First published by The Bodley Head, 1969

Puffin edition, 1971
This edition, 2013

1 3 5 7 9 10 8 6 4 2

Illustrations © The Bodley Head, 1969

These stories were originally taken from *Larky Legends*,
published by John Lane The Bodley Head (1938)

The right of Norman Hunter to be identified as the author of this work has been
asserted in accordance with the Copyright, Designs and Patents Act 1988.

The Random House Group Limited supports the Forest Stewardship Council® (FSC®),
the leading international forest-certification organisation. Our books carrying the FSC
label are printed on FSC®-certified paper. FSC is the only forest-certification scheme
supported by the leading environmental organisations, including Greenpeace. Our
paper procurement policy can be found at www.randomhouse.co.uk/environment.

Set in Bembo 13/15 pt

RANDOM HOUSE CHILDREN'S PUBLISHERS UK
61–63 Uxbridge Road, London W5 5SA

www.**randomhousechildrens**.co.uk
www.**totallyrandombooks**.co.uk
www.**randomhouse**.co.uk

Addresses for companies within The Random House Group Limited
can be found at: www.randomhouse.co.uk/offices.htm

THE RANDOM HOUSE GROUP Limited Reg. No. 954009

A CIP catalogue record for this book is available from the British Library.

Printed and bound by CPI Group (UK) Ltd, Croydon, CR0 4YY

*To my wife, who inspired some of the characters
in this book – the nice ones, of course.*

Contents

Foreword

(Explaining sort of talk that you
can skip if you like)

These stories are legends of the
future. In the ordinary way a legend
is a tale of something supposed to
have happened in the past. These
stories haven't happened yet but
perhaps one day they may. You
never know. Wouldn't it be fun if
they did?

NORMAN HUNTER

1

The Dribblesome Teapots

Tea was more than just an ordinary afternoon sort of affair in Sypso-Sweetleigh. It was positively a State function, yes it was. The King and Queen would as soon have thought of missing their own coronation as missing their tea.

There were eight kinds of bread and butter and sixteen kinds of cake, ranging from the very plain and wholesome to the terribly indigestible and delicious. The tea-service was of gold except the teapot, and that was a lovely big brown earthenware one, known as a Brown Betty. The Queen declared it was the only kind of pot that made good tea. It had the Royal arms on the inside as well as the outside because the Queen was so specially thorough she couldn't bear to think that things you didn't see weren't as nice as those you did. She always washed her neck much farther down than necessary; she insisted on all the cupboards being tidy inside and she even had her shoes polished on the soles, which was rather awkward sometimes because they made her slither about on the carpet. Still, she had learned to skate ages ago, so she managed to slither quite majestically.

'I declare I'm simply gasping for a cup of tea,' said Her Majesty one day when it was getting half-past fourish.

'My dear, ought you to gasp?' asked the King. He was known as King Nutherkupp II because that sounded nice and royal, but his real name was Leslie Jones. 'I mean to say,' he added, 'it isn't very majestic, is it?'

'It may not be very majestic,' said the Queen, 'but it is most exceedingly very true,' and she rang the bell for tea so hard that all the servants came hurrying in at once.

'Now, now, now,' said the Queen, 'I didn't ring for all of you. You know perfectly well I ring once for the Butler, twice for the footman, three times for the parlour-maids, four times for the Cook and so on.'

'Pardon, Majesty,' said the Butler, bowing so low that a clump of picture cards he was collecting from tea-packets fell out of his waistcoat pocket all over the floor and were picked up by the first and second footmen who were collecting the same set. 'Your Majesty rang so many times we were not quite sure if you were ringing once a lot of times, or twice not so many times, or three times several times, or . . .'

'Oh, go away, all of you,' cried the Queen, shooing them out like a lot of chickens. 'I rang for tea, and please hurry up with it.' She sat down and went on gasping to herself, while the King tried to make up his mind whether to have plain wholesome cake which was good for him, but which he didn't like, or delicious creamy pastries which he loved, but which gave him pains.

Then in came tea with the Butler all of a tremble, but trying not to show it because, most terrible of things to occur, he had chipped a bit off the spout of the Queen's Brown Betty!

'Perhaps Her Majesty won't notice it,' he thought. 'It's only a weeny little chip.' So he had rubbed a chocolate éclair on the chipped part to make it dark like the rest of the teapot and was hoping for the best and wondering how he could prepare for the worst, not knowing what the worst might be.

'Ah, tea at last,' said the Queen, brightening up, while the King suddenly made up his mind to have some of the plain wholesome cake first while he was hungry and then go on to the creamy pastries afterwards and hope that the plain wholesome cake would stop the pains that the creamy pastries gave him from being very noticeable.

The Queen began to pour out. And goodness gracious, how awful! The chipped spout of the Brown Betty made the tea dribble all over the tablecloth and all over her robes!

For a moment there was silence except for the drip, drip, drip of the tea on to the carpet. The Butler came over so queer that the footman gave him back the tea-packet cards, but still he felt no better.

'O-o-o-o-oh, disgraceful,' screamed the Queen, jumping up and putting the teapot down with such a bang that three lumps of sugar jumped out of the bowl into the King's tea; which he didn't at all mind because the Queen would never give him enough sugar anyway.

'Look at my lovely robes,' moaned the Queen, 'and oh, look at my lovely tablecloth, the one that Aunt Chrissie made for me with her own hands too! Not that she could have made it with anybody else's hands, but oh dear me, I shall cry, I know I shall.'

But she didn't cry, she went on talking and wailing and moaning and wringing her hands while the footmen began wringing the tablecloth to get the dribbled-over tea out of it. But alas and alack, they wrung it over the King's cake and made it all squodgy so that he had to have creamy pastries after all, pains or no pains, though it was pains all right as it turned out. Not that it was all right, him having pains, you know, but neither was it the least bit all right the Queen's teapot going all dribbly like that.

'If there's one thing I cannot stand, it's a teapot that dribbles,' cried the Queen. 'Oh, and that one was such a beautiful pourer. I can't understand what can have happened.'

The Butler could understand perfectly well, but he simply dared not tell the Queen about chipping the spout. So he said, 'I will fetch another teapot, Majesty.'

He fetched the best silver pot that was never used. But that was so ancient, having been part of the crown jewels of Sypso-Sweetleigh or something for years and years, that it was full of holes and dribbled in all directions instead of only at the spout.

'Oh, get me a teapot that doesn't dribble!' cried the Queen, gasping more than ever for her tea and not caring whether it was majestic or otherwise.

'Er – er – yes, Majesty,' said the Butler.

He brought the kitchen teapot, which was enamel and always had dribbled, only the Cook always held a bit of sponge under it. He brought a toy teapot from the little princess's toy cupboard, but that had no spout, and he brought two little ornamental sort of teapots with 'A present from Brighton' written on them and which didn't dribble because they were solid right through so weren't any more use than if they had.

'Oh, oh, oh, oh! this is terrible,' cried the Queen. 'Not a teapot in the Palace that can be used. Oh, disgraceful! I must have a teapot that doesn't dribble, I must, I must. Half the kingdom reward for anyone who can bring me a teapot that pours without dribbling!'

'Here, here, here, half a mo!' cried the King, getting all flurried and agitated and forgetting to speak regally. 'You can't do that. What do you think's going to happen to Sypso-

Sweetleigh if you go offering half of it for teapots?'

But it was too late. The Royal Herald who was a fearfully anxious-to-please sort of person had dashed out the minute the Queen said 'half the kingdom for a teapot that pours without dribbling', and before he could be caught and told to stop he had shouted the proclamation all round the city.

'Oh dear, oh dear, now you have done it, you have,' cried the King. 'Half the kingdom for a teapot! Oh, it's awful! As if you couldn't have gone up the road and bought another teapot. Those proclamation and reward sort of businesses are only meant for getting the kingdom saved from dragons and things like that. I do wish you'd be more careful.'

But the Queen wasn't listening. She'd gone away to change her robes while the Cook poured her out a cup of tea in the garden where the dribbles didn't matter and brought it in to her with the saucer over the cup.

The Butler, in despair at having caused such a to-do and a commotion, went straight to the Court Magician for advice, and hadn't been there more than two minutes when the King came in too, so he had to go out again without knowing whether the Magician could do anything about anything or not.

'This is terrible,' said the King; 'the Queen has offered half the kingdom for a teapot that pours without dribbling and the proclamation is all over the town. What can we do? Can't you un-proclamate it or something?'

'Alas, no, Majesty,' said the Court Magician, offering the King a pack of cards and asking him to take one and not say which one it was. But the King couldn't be bothered with conjuring sort of things, so smacked the cards up into the air in a shower where they all turned into birds and flew out of the window, except the one that the Magician was going to make the King take, and that became a piece of gingerbread which the Magician swallowed at one go while smoke came out of his ears.

'Well, well, you must do something about it, you know,' said the King. 'What's the use of a Court Magician if he can't do an impossibility or so now and again for the good of the country?'

'Well,' said the Magician, 'these things have to be thought out very carefully, you know, and sometimes one can get round a thing one can't do by doing several things one can do. For instance, supposing Your Majesty had been magicked and had three heads and came to me to make you have one head again; well, I couldn't do it, but what I could do would be to turn you into a newspaper, and then back into a king with only one head.'

'I see,' said the King, who didn't see at all really and began to think magic was a bit overrated.

'Depend upon me, Majesty,' said the Magician, producing a cup of cocoa from his hat and beginning to sip it. 'I will find a way to save the kingdom.'

So the King had to be satisfied with that, and the Magician sat up all night reading the most unlikely books and practising unheard-of incantations.

The next morning the grounds of the Palace were packed with people. It was like Lord Mayor's Show Day and Boat Race Day and Cup Final and Coronation Day and Royal Garden Party and Opening of Parliament all at once. Everybody in the kingdom seemed to be there. And everybody had brought at least one teapot; most of them had brought several and one or two of them had brought simply cartloads of teapots. There were teapots of every size, shape and colour. Enormous teapots for the most extensive tea-parties and tiny little personal teapots for tea in bed. Some of the teapots didn't even look like teapots and one that did look most extravagantly like a teapot wasn't a teapot at all, but a tremendous imitation one as big as a bath that used to hang outside the chief tea shop.

'There now,' exclaimed the King, 'now do you see what you've done with your offer of half the kingdom for a teapot? Look at them! All with teapots. And unless I'm greatly mistaken practically every one of those teapots will pour without dribbling and how we're going to give away absolutely hundreds of halves of kingdoms and what we're going to do with absolutely hundreds of teapots with none of the kingdom left to put them in I do not know. It's terrible!'

'Oh, but can't we say we've changed our minds,' said the Queen, 'and give them all a bag of oranges and send them home?'

'Bag of oranges!' snorted the King. 'And do you suppose that people who have come here with teapots hoping to get half the kingdom will go home quietly with bags of oranges? Why, there'd be a revolution or something. Not that it makes much difference,' he added gloomily. 'Something dreadful will come of this anyway. I don't see how it can help itself.'

His Majesty went downstairs and consulted with the Prime Minister.

'There's only one thing to do, Majesty,' said the Prime Minister. 'We must let them all bring their teapots in and make tea in them and see if they pour without dribbling.'

'Yes, and suppose they all pour without dribbling?' asked the King, throwing out his hands and hunching up his shoulders and raising his eyebrows all at once.

The Prime Minister didn't get a chance to answer that, for just then in swept the Queen.

'Now then,' she said firmly, 'I'm going to find a teapot that doesn't dribble whatever else happens. Tell them to bring in their teapots.'

So the people began to come in with their teapots. The first pot was handed to the King, who gave it to the Butler, who made tea in it and handed it to the Queen, who poured out from it.

It dribbled all over the place!

More tea was made in the second pot and that dribbled worse than the first.

And the third and fourth and fifth and sixth and goodness knows how many teapots had tea made in them and tea poured from them, and goodness gracious, would you believe it, they all dribbled. Yes, they did, every single one of them. Some of the big pots dribbled more than some of the little pots and some of the little pots dribbled more than the big ones. Some of them dribbled to the left and some to the right and some all ways at once.

'Thank goodness!' exclaimed the King to himself. 'Oh, if only they all dribble we're saved.'

By this time the pots were being filled with tea and poured out a dozen or so at a time, the footmen and parlour-maids helping the Queen, and holding three pots in each hand. But still they dribbled. The floor was swimming in tea. The Prime Minister took off his shoes and stockings to save them getting wet. Everywhere was getting as squishy as squishy.

'Oh dear, oh dear, this is awful,' sobbed the Queen. 'Oh, shan't I ever get a teapot that doesn't dribble?'

At last, every single teapot had been tried and every single one dribbled most horribly. The people went home all disappointed and puzzled and made themselves tea at home and found that their teapots poured out quite all right without dribbling. It was most mysterious.

'Well,' said the King, as the last person left the Palace, 'that saves the kingdom anyway, though I must say it seems to have ruined the carpet.'

'But my teapot, oh, my teapot,' wailed the Queen. 'Oh, I'd do anything to have a teapot that pours without dribbling.'

'Your Majesty,' said a voice.

They all turned. It was the Magician.

'Listen,' he said in his most magishy voice, 'the reason Your Majesty's Brown Betty dribbled was because the Butler quite accidentally chipped a weeny bit off the spout.'

'Oh!' gasped the Queen. 'Off with his head,' she shouted, but the King very hurriedly said, 'No, no, shush, please wait a minute,' only just in time to prevent the Herald rushing off for the Executioner.

'I couldn't magic the proclamation away once it had been proclamated. There are some things even a magician can't do, and that is one of them,' went on the Magician. 'So in order to save the kingdom from being given away in halves all over the place, I laid a spell on all the teapots in the kingdom to make them dribble.'

'Oh !' said the Queen again, and she was just going to cry 'Off with his head' when she remembered it wasn't much good offing with a magician's head because he'd have just put it back again.

'Now, Your Majesty,' continued the Magician, 'I'm sure you will realize that the Butler didn't mean to chip the Brown Betty teapot, and if you promise not to do anything nasty to him I will just do a small magic and mend the Brown Betty so that it will pour without dripping.'

'Yes, yes, I promise,' said the Queen eagerly.

So the Brown Betty was brought in and the Magician did his small magic. Then tea was made in the Brown Betty.

'I bet it dribbles,' said the Prime Minister, who had begun to believe that all teapots would always dribble for evermore, he'd seen so many of them doing it.

The Queen picked up the Brown Betty and poured out a cup of tea.

The teapot didn't dribble so much as a spot!

She poured out cup after cup and not one dribble did the Brown Betty drib.

'Thank goodness for that,' exclaimed the King, and he went out for a nice game of croquet to calm himself down, while the Queen, who thought it rather a shame after all to have disappointed everybody about half the kingdom, had a coloured picture of herself

and the King sent to everyone who had brought a teapot. And some of them hung their picture in the dining-room and some in the bedroom. Some hung it upside down because they weren't sure which way it ought to go. (If *you* look at the picture upside down, you will see why they weren't sure.) And some kept it to frighten their children with when they were naughty, which wasn't very polite to the King and Queen, but then perhaps it wasn't a very good picture.

2

The Priceless Present

If you could have been in the town of Kumdown Upwardz, the capital of Inkrediblania, one sunny afternoon – which you couldn't have because it's too far away – you would have heard cheers and seen waving of flags as a horseman rode down the main street to the Royal Palace.

'Hurray,' cried everyone. 'Hip, hip, hoojolly-well-ray,' and they threw roses at him and those who hadn't any roses threw kisses instead. You would have thought it was the King of Inkrediblania himself, but it wasn't. It was Count Beeniwunnum Harteigh, the best-loved man in the kingdom and one of the poorest. He had nearly everything except money. He had a handsome face and nice manners and a kind heart. And he was very clever. He could jump fences backwards on his horse, make oranges disappear so that nobody knew where they had gone and invent the most exciting games on the spur of the moment. No wonder everybody liked him. He was as nice and generous as the King was horrid and mean, but the King can wait a bit while the people of Kumdown Upwardz are throwing their roses and kisses at the Count. It isn't often you can keep a king waiting and as this one isn't a very nice king, we may as well make him wait while we've got the chance.

At last all the roses were thrown and most of the kisses, and the Count jumped off his horse in front of the Palace, while the people went on cheering and dancing about.

'Oh, bother,' said the King, looking through the window, 'here's that Beeniwunnum Harteigh chap again. Now what can he want this time? Come to borrow the lawn-mower, I suppose, or to ask himself to tea.' The King disliked the Count because he was so popular with the populace.

'Oh, how can you, my dear?' said the Queen, who was all for peace and not quarrelling with anyone, because she liked a nice quiet life and plenty of lavender among the linen. You know the sort of queen she was. The sort it's nice to have as an aunt if you're lucky enough. 'You know he never borrows the lawn-mower,' she went on, 'and he certainly never asks himself to tea.'

'Pah,' snorted the King, a very difficult thing to do unless you practise it a lot, which the King did, because it was so useful for stopping people saying things he didn't want to hear.

'His Goodness Graciousness Count Beeni-wunnum Harteigh,' announced the Butler.

'Your Majesties,' said the Count, bowing so low that his coat nearly fell off over his head, 'I come to ask a favour.'

'What did I tell you?' growled the King under his breath, then aloud, 'Well, what is it?'

'I – er – er – I, well, the fact is,' said the Count, getting all nervous, 'you see, I, that is to say we, or rather if you would—'

'That's all right,' said the Queen, smiling at him, 'we quite understand.'

'We do nothing of the kind,' said the King. 'Do you want to borrow the lawn-mower or what?'

That made the Count so nervous that he nearly said yes although he did not want to borrow the lawn-mower, which would have been silly because he had no lawn to mow, and anyway what he wanted to ask was something much more important. He wanted to ask for the hand of the King's daughter, Princess Joyday, in marriage. But he got so nervous and tied up about it that at last he had to write it down on a piece of paper and give it to the King.

'What!' roared the King when he had read it, only ever so much louder than that. 'How dare you, sir! To ask for the hand of the Princess! Impudence! Disgraceful! I'm surprised at you! *Pah!*' and His Majesty jumped up and tramped up and down in front of the throne, nearly treading on the Queen's feet only she managed to get them out of the way each time.

'But, my dear,' she said, putting a hand on

the King's arm as he went by, 'why shouldn't he marry Joyday? He's handsome and clever and nice.'

'Handsome!' snapped the King. 'Clever! Nice!' Each word shot out of his mouth as if it had been fired from a cannon and at each word all the courtiers gave a jump. 'What have those things to do with it? This is no mere matter of lawn-mowers. Marry Joyday, indeed! Pah!' The King was so mean that he was determined to marry his daughter to someone tremendously rich and, of course, the Count was tremendously poor, so altogether it didn't look as if he was going to have much chance.

'Pardon me, Your Majesty,' said the Lord Chamberlain at that moment, 'but there is a law of Inkrediblania, which says that if anyone asks for the hand of the Princess in marriage he must be given some test to perform and if he succeeds in the test he wins the Princess.'

The Count cheered up a bit at this. He was very good at tests and puzzles and things.

'What a silly law,' said the King.

'Ah, but, Your Majesty,' whispered the Lord Chamberlain very craftily, 'it is a most fortunate law. The thing is to give him a test that he can't possibly do, then he can't marry the Princess and everything's all right.'

'Oh, yes, of course, fancy my not thinking of that,' said the King, and the Count continued to feel cheerful, because he hadn't heard the last part.

'Well, Count,' went on the King, 'if you really want to marry the Princess you must first be put to the test. If you fail you lose the Princess and your head as well.' There was nothing in the law about losing heads, but the King put that in to make it harder because he disliked the Count.

'I am ready, Majesty,' said the Count, wondering what the test would be and going through his multiplication tables very quickly in case it was anything about how many things made what.

The King and the Lord Chamberlain whispered together again; it wasn't good manners to whisper in company really, but kings may do as they like and whispering may have been polite in Inkrediblania, you never know.

Presently they stopped whispering; the Lord Chamberlain scratched his ear where the King's chin had been tickling him.

'We have decided,' said the King, 'that the test is to be this—'

Everyone listened with bated breath except those who were out of breath from excitement and they just listened with their ears.

'—If you can bring to me within a week,' said the King, 'a present as valuable as the Princess herself, you may marry her. Fail, and off comes your head. My decision is final and no competitor may win more than one prize.' He didn't mean to say the last bit, but he'd read it in a competition in the *Inkrediblania Times* and it slipped out by accident.

'Heavens!' thought the Count, 'I am undone. The Princess is priceless, I know she is. Whatever I bring cannot be so valuable as she and I can't afford anything valuable anyway.' But before he'd had time to finish thinking all that the King's guards hustled him about slightly and got him outside without seeming to have pushed him. Then they all saluted clickety-clicket-click and went in again slamming the Palace door behind them; while the King was so proud of having set the Count such a hopeless sort of test that he swelled out his chest and burst all the buttons off his waistcoat.

'What is more valuable than the Princess?' said the Count to himself for the three hundred and goodness knows how manyth time, but he couldn't think of the answer. He scratched his head. He rang for his servants and scratched their heads. They scratched each other's heads. They went out and scratched up the garden. But still none of them could think what could be more valuable than the Princess.

Then the Count looked up the question in his encyclopaedia, but couldn't find it. He looked up the word princess, and found it meant king's daughter, which he knew already. He looked up priceless and found it means without price and that didn't help. He looked up present and found it meant 'see also gift', so he looked up gift and found it meant present.

'This is terrible,' he cried, flipping the leaves over in a shower without bothering to look any more. 'There isn't anything as valuable as the Princess and yet there's got to be or I lose my head and the Princess too. Oh, what sort of a present can I give to the King that's priceless and yet doesn't cost anything?

'I could go in and say, "I give your Majesty good morning," but would that count? Perhaps a good morning isn't as valuable as the Princess, though? It doesn't last so long, anyway.'

No, that wouldn't do, he would have to think of something else. Suppose he gave the King a cold? No, that would have nothing to do with anything. Suppose he gave His Majesty a bottle of medicine to bring him good health? Good health was surely as valuable as the Princess, because where would she herself be without it? 'No, no,' said the Count, as soon as he'd thought of it. 'Princes in fairy tales might get away with some sort of dodge like that, but the King wouldn't have it. I know he wouldn't. He's the sort of king who won't have anything if he can help it.'

He went on thinking and some of the servants came in to ask if they could stop scratching their heads as it hurt and they couldn't think any better by doing it. But he was thinking so hard he didn't hear them, so some of them left off scratching their heads and some went on, which wasn't really fair, but I don't see that it mattered. Not when the Count hadn't thought of the priceless present.

'What can I give him, what can I give him?' groaned the Count. He began looking at magazines to see if he could get an idea from them. He got several ideas for new ways to plant the garden, two or three ideas for new colours to paint the roof and any number of new ideas for what to do with left-over scraps from Sunday's joint. But they didn't interest him because he had no garden, very little roof and hardly ever a Sunday joint.

'Suppose I give him a present with the price ticket taken off,' he thought. 'That would be priceless. But no, the King said the present must be as valuable as the Princess, he didn't say anything about priceless. It was I who thought of that. Clever of me, but it doesn't help much. Supposing I – supposing – a, oo-er. Good heavens! Dare I do it? Yes. No. Perhaps. What if I don't? Lose head. Lose Princess. Shall I risk it? Might come off. Who knows? Ha—'

That was the Count getting an idea at last. But it was such a ninety-miles-an-hour sort of idea he hardly dared to think about it.

'If it fails I lose my head and the Princess,' he said. 'If I don't try it I lose them anyway. Might as well try – and run like anything if it doesn't work.' So he set to work to make his plans.

The last day of the test had arrived. Before

nightfall the Count must hand the King a present as valuable as the Princess, or lose his head. Which would he do? The populace was agog with excitement, even those who didn't know what agog meant were agog with it. They couldn't help themselves.

'He'll never do it, Your Majesty,' said the crafty Lord Chamberlain, who had suggested the impossible test to the King. 'You will be rid of him for ever, ha, ha!'

The King smiled and rubbed his hands. 'For ever,' he murmured.

'Then why not let me marry the Princess?' said the Lord Chamberlain. 'I have gold. I have jewels. I have land.'

'And you have a nasty face and a lot of impudence,' put in the Queen, who had just arrived and heard what he said. 'Joyday doesn't love you and you know it.'

'Tut, tut, my dear,' said the King, 'I am not sure that our good Chamberlain would not after all be the most suitable husband in the kingdom for Joyday.'

'If you dare permit it,' said the Queen, 'I shall—'

But they never heard what she would do,

for just at that moment trumpets sounded, doors flew open, servants flew about.

'His Goodness Graciousness Count Beeniwunnum Harteigh,' announced the Butler, and in came the Count followed by two servants carrying a big carved wooden chest.

'Your Majesty,' he said, 'I have brought a present as valuable as the Princess.'

'You've what?' shouted the King. 'Where did you get it?'

'I must admit, Your Majesty,' said the Count, 'that I stole it.'

'You stole it,' shrieked the King, getting so angry that his crown went up and down slightly on top of his head. 'You stole it and you have the impudence, the outrageous impudence, sir, to dare to come here and offer a stolen present to your King. Pah! I refuse to accept it. Take it away, whatever it is.'

'But what shall I do with it?' asked the Count.

'Give it back to the person you stole it from,' said the King.

'I have already offered it to him, but he refuses to take it back, Your Majesty,' said the Count.

The King scratched his head and thought for a bit, while the Count looked on and thought how nice it was to see someone else scratching his head and thinking and not having to do it himself.

'Then if the person you stole this present from refuses to take it back, the only thing I can say is you had better keep it,' said the King, 'but you can't give it to me as a way of winning the Princess. Oh, no, no, no!'

'Your Majesty,' cried the Count and his voice boomed out like an organ. 'The test is finished. It no longer exists. Your Majesty has already given me the Princess.' He clapped his hands and the servants stood by the chest they had brought in.

'Behold,' cried the Count, 'the present which is the only thing as valuable as the Princess.' The lid of the chest flew up and out stepped the Princess herself.

'Explain everything,' gasped the King, who had collapsed on to the throne like a balloon with a pin stuck in it when the Princess appeared.

'Certainly,' said the Count. 'I stole the Princess from you this morning. I offered her to you just now and you said you wouldn't accept a present I had stolen. You told me to give it back to the person I took it from. I told your Majesty that

I had offered it to him and he wouldn't take it. That was true because I offered her to you. You told me in that case I could keep the present I had stolen. The present was the Princess. There is nothing else in the kingdom so valuable as she unless it be the Queen,' he added with a graceful bow.

'And I don't count in this,' said the Queen, jumping up and taking the Count's hand. 'Bravo, Count, the Princess is yours. Clever man. Come on now, Herbert,' – she turned to the King – 'you can't get out of it, you've given the Princess to the Count and they're going to be married. Tell the Lord Chamberlain to send out the invitations and have the confetti got out.'

So the Count and the Princess were married and the wicked Lord Chamberlain made such a mess of sending out the invitations that he was dismissed and had to go and grow onions which he disliked because they made him cry. And the Count became Lord Chamberlain himself and a very good one he was too, because he was so clever he thought of all sorts of ways to make ruling the kingdom rather easier than falling off a chair and considerably more pleasant.

3

The Unexpected Banquet

There were no calendars in the Kingdom of Sundimundee, because printing hadn't been invented. So a man used to go round with a different-coloured ribbon tied round his arm according to what day it was. He had a red ribbon for Mondays, a green one for Tuesdays, a blue one for Wednesdays, and so on. And everybody had only to look at his ribbon to know at once whether it was early closing day, or half-holiday or bath night, or the day for cleaning out the spare room, and so on.

And, of course, the man with the ribbon was a most important and valuable official. In fact he was really one of the Weather Clerk's assistants who had been lent to the King for the purpose.★

'There's an awful lot of illness about just

★ This part of the story isn't so extreme as it sounds. In Siam the people really did wear a sort of sash the colour of which was different for each day of the week. But, of course, that doesn't account for what happens next.

now, my dear,' said the King to the Queen. 'We ought to send the man who wears the day ribbons down to be vaccinated. It would be awful if he caught anything. Nobody would know where they were or whether they had passed it or if it was too late or much too early or even if everything was anything.'

'Yes, yes,' said the Queen, hoping the King wasn't going on talking muddly sort of things like that because it made her forget where she was with the lace piano cover she was making.

So the Days' Man was sent along to the Court Physician and vaccinated that very day.

But, oh dear, the silly-not-thinking sort of person, whatever must he go and do but tie a red ribbon round his vaccinated arm so people shouldn't bump into it and hurt him. Yes, and a red ribbon meant Monday and this was Wednesday. There! Everything the King had said might happen if he was ill looked like happening because he wasn't.

'Monday already,' said everyone, scratching their heads or their noses, or their chins, according to what sort of people they were. 'This has been a most short week.' Which, of course, it was, but there was the Days' Man strutting about with a red Monday ribbon on his arm, so Monday it had to be and no use arguing.

So all the shopkeepers who'd thought it was Wednesday and shut their shops for early closing had to open them again. And all the school children who'd got all ready to stay at home for half-holiday had to go to school again. And extra bath nights were got ready for and spare rooms were cleaned out again, though they didn't need it.

But none of that would really have mattered so frightfully much if it hadn't been that the King and Queen were giving a magnificent banquet to all the important people in the kingdom on the Monday that was still to come, but which everyone thought was here already. So, of course, all those important people put on their most important clothes and hung their important jewels round their important selves and all got delivered in coaches and things at the Royal Palace.

'Agnes, Agnes, quick, come here!' cried the King, when he caught sight of them through the throne-room window. 'People arriving for the banquet. Is it Monday? Can't be. Monday was the other day. What shall we do?'

'What's this? What's this?' cried the Queen,

rushing in with her nose only half powdered and with ten maids following her down the stairs trying to do her dress up as she ran but not managing to do it. 'Banquet! Tonight! Impossible! What day is it?'

She threw a glance out of the window looking for the Days' Man, but as he wasn't there, the glance went right round the garden and came back to her again without doing any good.

'Quick!' she cried, grasping the situation with her womanly intuition and her queenly brain and her royal readiness all at once. 'Go and tell them funny stories, Kingy, while I get something started,' and she dashed off to the kitchen, with the maids still following, but not bothering about trying to do up her dress any more as she was pulling it off in order to put on a nice big apron.

'Cook,' she cried, 'guests have arrived for the banquet. It's Monday and nobody told us.'

'Heavens, mum, I mean, Majesty,' said the Cook, going all pale and shutting the book she was reading without marking the place. 'There's nothing in the house, I should say Palace, mum – er –Majesty. Nothing except a tin of sardines or so.'

'Bring out your sardines,' said the Queen,

flourishing a rolling-pin. 'There's got to be a banquet tonight by hook or by crook, or by anything else you like. Some sort of a banquet, any sort of a banquet, but a banquet.' She lit the gas oven which went bang right in her face, dropped the rolling-pin on the Cook's toe, turned on both the water taps and grabbed the biggest bowl.

'Bring out everything eatable and anything that looks as if it might be eatable,' she commanded, tying a yellow duster round her hair. And the maids who weren't kitchen maids at all, but dressing-boudoir-bedroom sort of maids had to tie teacloths round their middles and get things out and put them away again and rush about helping, though they didn't help much because they weren't used to making banquets but only beds.

While all this was going on the King had gone to greet the noble and noticeable visitors and was trying to keep them amused with funny stories until the Queen could let him know that the banquet was ready by ringing a bell.

'I wonder,' said the King in his best telling a story manner, 'if you know the story of the man who – er that is to say the lady from – or rather I should say the way in which ...' But nobody knew that one and as the King couldn't remember it either they didn't hear it.

Then the King talked a lot and was just going to have a shot at singing a song when a bell rang.

'Thank goodness,' breathed the King inside his beard, 'the banquet's ready.' But it wasn't. The bell was a muffin man's, but the King didn't discover it till too late and everyone was sitting round the table waiting for something to happen. So he had to have yet another shot at a story and this time he'd nearly finished it when he remembered he'd forgotten the last bit where it makes you laugh. But it didn't matter for just then 'Br-r-r-r-ing' went a bell and in came the Queen.

'We've made a sort of a banquet out of the most unlikely kind of scraps,' whispered the Queen to the King as she sat down. 'Goodness knows what everyone will think, but let's hope they won't. Whatever you do, don't eat a crumb or there won't be enough to go round.'

Then in came the servants carrying the first course. Everyone got something different. One duke got a sardine-and-a-half on a biscuit-and-a-half and started doing sums to see how much more he'd have if he'd had twice as much as half of what was missing. A duchess got one pickle, one top half of a slice off a cottage loaf, and three assorted peanuts. The Prime Minister received a lettuce leaf wrapped daintily round a piece of orange with a dab of mustard on it, and the Lord Chief Justice had the pink icing off an almond finger laid carefully on top of a stewed plum. One of the marchionesses was given ten little dog biscuits by mistake through one of the maids having taken the Queen's dog's breakfast, which he hadn't eaten, thinking it was part of the banquet, and the Lord Chancellor had a very generous portion of damp teacloth that the Cook had left on a plate and which oughtn't to have been brought in at all.

'Charming weather, don't you think, and so much of it,' said the King, clattering his knife and fork about ever so much on an empty plate because he hadn't been given anything to eat.

'You must let me give you the pattern of a simply too sweet jumper, my dear,' said the Queen to the most important duchess, who was doing her best with a brazil nut and half a cold sausage and trying to look as if she liked them.

Then the servants came and cleared away the plates for the next course. All the guests had left something on their plates just for manners

and several of them had left everything, either
because they didn't like it or because they
couldn't eat it, or because they were so aston-
ished at having such unlikely food served at a
Royal Banquet that they hadn't time to start
before their plates were taken away again.

'Whatever are you going to do for the next
course?' whispered the King.

'Shush,' said the Queen. 'You wait.'

Presently in came the next course, and what do you think it was? Why, the servants had taken all the left-over bits from the first course and mixed them up and served them out again and brought them in for the second course. Everyone got something different from what they'd had before, only not quite so much, except the Lord Chancellor who got the damp teacloth again.

Then the King, who'd just been served with another plate full of nothing, stood up and said, 'My Lords, Ladies and Gentlemen, let us drink to the Kingdom of Sundimundee,' so of course everyone had to stand up to drink the toast, and immediately they stood up the servants whisked round ever so quickly and took all the plates away again with hardly anything eaten.

'This is more like a game of cards than a banquet,' said the Cook, splitting a bean left by a marquis into three and giving one piece each to a duchess, a baronet and a bishop.

Then in came the third course, made of what had been left of the second one, mixed up and dealt out differently again. And once more everyone got something different and still less of it than before. The Lord Chancellor got the damp teacloth again.

Then up popped the Queen to propose the health of the guests and as soon as everyone had sat down after drinking that the King jumped up and said, 'Here's to absent friends,' meaning those who hadn't been invited. So the servants were able to clear the plates again and get away with nearly everything they had brought in.

And all through the fourth and fifth and sixth courses that unreasonable sort of bewildering banquet went on. Each time the Cook mixed up what was left and shuffled it round again. Each time everyone got a little bit less until some of them were being given half a split pea or one end of a lentil. And all the time the King and Queen kept popping up and proposing the most extreme sort of toasts like 'Here's to the fire brigade,' and 'Let us drink the toast of the royal baker,' which sounded the most awful nonsense, but was the best they could do on the spur of the moment. Anyway it made the guests keep popping up too and gave the servants a chance to snatch their plates away with bits of food still on them, so as to make the banquet go another course or so.

But everyone was getting most alarmingly hungry. The King and Queen had been served with seven empty plates and had nothing on the eighth, none of which was very satisfying. Still they were too anxious to feel that they were hungry. But the guests who either didn't like what they got or weren't given time to eat it if they did, felt positively hollow inside themselves.

'Next time I go to a Royal Banquet I shall take sandwiches with me,' whispered a duke who'd just managed to swallow half an inch of macaroni before his plate was whisked away.

'Me, too,' said a marchioness, forgetting to speak correctly because she was so hungry.

'Gr-mph-mph-g-g-g,' said the Lord Chancellor who'd had the damp teacloth every time and at last had got so hungry he'd cut a piece off with his pocket scissors and was trying ever so desperately to eat it, but finding it rather a job.

Things were getting awful. The King and Queen couldn't think of any more toasts to propose and several guests had actually managed to eat something. Then the Butler sidled up to the Queen and whispered, 'There isn't anything more left to eat, your Majesty, except half a teaspoonful of cold gravy and three haricot beans, one with a piece missing, and they won't go round.'

'Ooer,' thought the Queen, but she was regal enough not to say it. 'Whatever can we do? A Royal Banquet has to last at least fourteen courses and we've only had nine.'

'Think of another toast, quick,' whispered the King, but they couldn't think of one, and some of the less noble guests were beginning to tap slightly on the table with their fingertips. If they didn't get something to eat soon they might start banging their spoons and forks about and that would be awful at a Royal Banquet.

Then all of a sudden there was a commotion at the doors and in rushed the Days' Man with a blue Wednesday ribbon round his arm and holding up the red Monday one.

'Your Majesties,' he cried. 'Oh, forgive me. Oh dear, oh dear.' And he told them all about how he'd tied the red ribbon round his vaccinated arm and everything.

'Then it *is* Wednesday,' said the Queen. 'I thought it was because my doggie never likes to have breakfast on Wednesdays and he didn't have any this morning.'

'Hum,' thought the marchioness who'd been given the ten little dog biscuits for the first course, but she was too polite to say anything and even if she hadn't been she wouldn't have had the chance to say it because the King jumped up and everyone grabbed their glasses and stood up too, thinking it was to be another toast. But it wasn't.

'My Lords, Ladies and Gentlemen,' said His Majesty, 'we're awfully sorry about this funny sort of banquet, but there's been a mistake. It isn't Monday, it's only Wednesday, and we weren't ready.' He told them how it had happened and everyone stood up and cheered, partly because they thought the King and Queen should be congratulated for trying so hard to give them a banquet, although it was the wrong day, and partly because the King said there would be a proper banquet on Monday as arranged.

'And now I think someone had better invent printing,' said the King, 'so that we can have calendars.' So someone did and they had them, so that sort of confusion isn't likely to happen any more.

4

The Queen Who Economized

Rather many giants and dragons had been ravishing the Kingdom of Simultania, so what with giving rewards here and prizes there and holding receptions and having banquets, the King and Queen found themselves absolutely short of money. Economies were the rule in the Palace. The King had given up his throne and was using a deck-chair instead, which looked rather odd but was quite comfortable. The Queen had given orders that crumpets were to be toasted on one side only, to save the gas. And by gradually making tea-time a bit later each day she had managed things so that nobody wanted any supper.

The King's nephew offered to give up washing.

'I've just thought of another way to econo-what-you-call-it,' said the Queen one day.

'Mize,' said the King, looking up from his book which he was reading slowly because he thought it would be cheaper, but really it was more expensive because he kept it out too long from the library.

'Mize?' said the Queen. 'You mean mice, don't you, and if so, what about them?'

'Mize, I said,' repeated the King. 'Economize, that's what you meant you had another idea for doing,' he went on, hoping it wasn't to be an idea for making him have less sugar in his tea, or not so much jam on his bread, or no treacle at all on his pudding.

'Listen,' said the Queen, 'I need some new robes.'

'That isn't econo-what's-a-naming,' cried the King. 'That isn't saving money. New robes indeed!'

'Oh, do listen a moment,' said the Queen. 'I'm not going to have any new robes.'

'Then what did you want to go saying you were for?' said the King, sinking back into his deck-chair throne, which suddenly collapsed flat and left him kicking about on the floor.

'I mean I need robes but I shan't have them,' said the Queen, getting all mixed up and starting to wave her hands about to make things easier, which it didn't. 'I mean I'm going to dry-clean my present ones with the petrol stuff they make motors go with.'

'Who do?' asked the King, getting up and starting the sort of tangled-up struggle with his deck-chair that he always had to have before he got it to stand up.

'Oh, they,' said the Queen. 'You know, motor people. They put the stuff in the motor somewhere, then they pull little handles and – chug-chug, toot-toot – off they go.'

'And a lot of help that will be to you with your robes,' said the King, getting his deck-chair set up backwards, but thinking it was the right way round.

'Oh, don't be so silly,' cried the Queen, stamping her foot but wishing she hadn't because she had a corn on it. 'I'm going to get some of that petrol stuff and . . .'

'Chug-chug, toot-toot, off we go,' cried the King, sitting down on his deck-chair and falling flat again at once.

But the Queen had gone.

Her Majesty had some rather botherishness about dry-cleaning the robes because she couldn't find anything big enough to swoosh them about in, except the bath, and even that wasn't quite big enough because the robes were rather wholesale and had long trailing pieces and big sleeves and all that regal business.

She was gazing gloomily out of the windows of the Palace wondering what to do when she caught sight of an ornamental pond in the grounds.

'Lovely,' she cried, having an idea.

'Most delightful,' agreed the King, who'd helped make the pond himself and was rather proud of it, although his helping only went as far as sticking a gold spade into the ground where the pond was to be and leaving the workmen to do the rest.

But the Queen didn't wait to hear him. She shot off downstairs and found the head gardener.

'Get all the water out of that pond,' she commanded, and away she went to the royal motor-house to get petrol.

The water was got out of the pond. Petrol was poured in. The Queen brought her robes along and flopped them in and began stirring them round with the second-best garden rake that had tissue-paper wound round it so that it shouldn't hurt the robes.

Flop, flop, swish – whoosh – flop, went the Queen with the robes. The King thought there looked room enough for something else so he dropped in the tea-cosy Cousin Binnie had given the Queen which immediately got itself stuck on the end of the rake and wouldn't come off.

Flop, flop, swish – whoosh – flop.

The King's nephew who felt dreadfully un-patriotic over not being allowed to give up washing for the good of the kingdom, was off practising killing dragons in case any came along. He'd made a dummy dragon out of some old clothes of the Queen's, stuffed out with straw. The head of his dragon was a boot-box, with a photograph of the King stuck on the front because that was the fiercest-looking thing the nephew could find, there not being any of the

Queen. And to make it look really fiery he had put a row of candles in its mouth and lit them. It didn't look frightfully fiery, but still it looked somewhat fiery, as long as you half-closed your eyes and didn't expect too much.

'Have at thee, cruel brrrrute,' cried the nephew, thinking that was how dragon-slaying people spoke. Then he snorted twice for the dragon because the dragon couldn't snort, and drawing his bow to its fullest extent he let fly arrow after arrow at the dummy dragon.

The first arrow missed and hit the Lord Chamberlain who was having a slight doze near by. The second arrow went a bit closer but still missed and scared the Queen's dog who was looking for a stick to get fierce with but didn't

seem to like the idea of getting fierce with an arrow. But the third struck the dummy dragon bonk! right on the boot-box and carried it away, candles and all, over the trees, splash! right into the ornamental pond full of petrol that the Queen was cleaning her robes in. And of course the lighted candles made it all blow absolutely up, with a whoosh and a bang like every Guy Fawkes' day in history going off at once.

A jet of flame shot seemingly miles into the air. The Queen's robes which had gone nearly clean were immediately clean gone. So was the King's cousin's tea-cosy which didn't matter because nobody liked it. The people of Simultania thought it must be a dragon worse than any they had ever seen and dashed simultaneously into their cellars, getting stuck in the doorways in their hurry.

'Her Majesty'll be spoiling her robes if she flops them about as loudly as that,' said the King to the Prime Minister. He was inside the Palace and thought the bang was part of the Queen's flopping business with the robes.

But he didn't think it for long, for at that moment the Queen herself, with one eyebrow blown off, came in backwards through the window without stopping to open it. Crash

bang, tinkle tinkle. 'Do you call this econo—' began the King.

'Help, help,' screamed the Queen. 'Awful bang, dragons or something, help!'

The King dashed out trying to draw his sword, but forgetting that he'd sold his real sword to pay the grocer's bill and was making do with a dummy kind of sword that couldn't be drawn. Into the grounds he dashed, followed not too closely by the Prime Minister and absolutely distantly by the nephew who guessed there might be some trouble about things.

'Gracious!' exclaimed His Majesty, stopping so suddenly that the Prime Minister ran bump into him.

The pond had gone. In its place was a huge

hole. Most untidy. But ha, ha! Yes, ha, absolutely ha! What was that at the bottom of the hole? The King sprang in and fell over. Was it gold? You bet it was! The ancient treasure of Simultania, hidden goodness knows when and up till that minute nobody knew where, was revealed!

'Hurray!' yelled the King, 'the kingdom is rich again!'

'Now I can have some new robes after all,' cried the Queen, coming out from behind the door where she was hiding in case it was a dragon.

The King had his proper throne back, but could never bring himself to sink really luxuriously into it again because he was always afraid it might go flat.

The crumpets were toasted on both sides again. Tea-time was put back and supper came into fashion once more. The nephew was forgiven, but had to keep on washing, and the Queen had a false eyebrow to wear in place of the one that was blown off. Nobody noticed it except when she was surprised and then only her real eyebrow went up and the false one stayed where it was. But the kingdom was rich again, so what did it matter?

5

The King with the Paper Face

The Imperial Physician of Astufflavia came out of the King's bedroom with a very serious look on his face and a very comic hat in his hand.

'His Majesty,' he began in a very bowed-down voice, dabbing his forehead nervously with a small flag of the Astufflavian Navy which he had taken from his pocket in mistake for a handkerchief, 'has Astufflavian measles and must not leave his room for five weeks.' He drew himself up, clapped his comic hat on backwards by mistake and strode down the corridor, kicking up the mats like anything.

'Alas,' groaned the Prime Minister, 'we are undone,' and the other not-so-Prime-Ministers who were waiting in the corridor echoed 'undone' in very underdone voices and held themselves together as well as they could in the face of such trying circumstances.

Here was the King laid up with Astufflavian measles for five weeks and the Most Frightfully

Grand Congress of the Seven Nations that is held only once in every thousand years was due to be held in Astufflavia that very week!

It was enough to make the Primest Minister quail to be had on toast like that.

King Watitizit of Astufflavia lay languidly on his royal couch and gazed mournfully at the ceiling which he couldn't see because it was too dark.

'Oh dear, my measles,' he said, 'and oh dear, the Congress. I don't know which is worrying me the most.'

Astufflavian measles are very nasty things to have. Instead of getting little red spots all over you like ordinary measles you get one big red spot about the size of a coconut on top of your head. But that goes after the second day and you feel quite all right and fearfully hungry and aren't allowed to have anything to eat except breadcrumbs for five weeks.

'I'm so sorry,' said the Queen who was at his bedside and had resolved to stay by him whatever happened. She'd had Astufflavian measles when she was little and couldn't get them again, you see. 'It's too bad you should get ill just when this Congress is coming off. Couldn't I go instead?'

'Impossible,' groaned the King, reaching out for one of the grapes his aunt had sent him, but the Queen had eaten them all. 'I must be there myself or the Judwallah of Istapampam will preside and decide all sorts of things I don't want decided and mess things up no end.'

'Gentlemen,' said the Prime Minister at lunch-time that day, pushing away his plate with the fifth helping of chocolate blancmange only half-finished, 'something must be done about this. His Majesty simply must preside at the Congress. What can we do?'

'Can't we put the Congress off until the King is well again?' asked one of the ministers.

'Impossible,' said the Prime Minister. 'Many of the monarchs are already on their way. The Emperor of Empirico started yesterday. The Nabob of Notsofast started the day before and a message has come from the Judwallah of Ista-pampam, the most powerful sovereign of all next to the King of Astufflavia, saying that he would have been here already only he's had a puncture. It's terrible,' he went on. 'Think of the important questions to be settled at the Congress.'

'There is the question of whether rhubarb

is a fruit or a vegetable,' said the Minister of Agriculture, passing his plate for more of it, whichever it was.

'And the question of whether people can buy acid drops on Wednesday afternoons,' added the Minister of the Interior with two of them in his mouth.

'And the question of how many beans make five and whether you can do it with jumping beans,' put in the Minister of Education.

The Prime Minister stood up.

'There is only one way out of the difficulty,' he said. 'We must have another king!'

Another king! The ministers gasped all together and swayed backwards all together and would have fallen flat on their backs all together at this monstrous suggestion if they hadn't all caught hold of the tablecloth all together to steady themselves.

'Oh, I don't mean what you mean,' said the Prime Minister hurriedly, grabbing at his half-finished plate of blancmange as it went sailing away from him on the cloth that the ministers had caught hold of. 'I mean we must make an imitation king, put him in the Council Chamber and pretend it is His Majesty.'

'That's a great idea,' said the Minister of

Agriculture, 'and we could dress him in the King's second-best robes.'

'Housekeeper will lend us some brooms and sticks and things for his body and we can pad him out with pillows,' said the Minister of the Interior, getting quite excited and swallowing both his acid drops at once.

'And we can paint a face on a piece of paper to make it look like him,' said the Minister of Education, who was taking lessons in painting and had just bought a brand-new paint-box costing goodness knows how many Astufflavian shillings.

'It's a wow,' said the Prime Minister, using the Astufflavian dialect in his excitement; 'come on and find the housekeeper,' and off they went leaving the tablecloth half on the floor.

They got a mop for the head and tied the crown on with string at the back where it wouldn't show. Then they tied pillows round the handle of the mop and over them put the King's second-best robes, the blue and gold ones with the Astufflavian alligators embroidered on the front. They tied an umbrella on one side for an arm and a walking-stick the other side, while a rolling-pin and a garden rake did very well for legs, even though one was a bit shorter than the other.

'He won't have to walk so it doesn't matter,' said the Prime Minister.

Then they put a pair of the King's riding-boots on the dummy and last of all a paper face painted with the Minister of Education's new paint-box. And when the dummy king was finished and propped up on the throne he looked more like the King than the King himself did.

Just then a page came hurrying into the room.

'Please, sir, the Judwallah of What's-his-name has come,' he stuttered.

'We had better receive him in the yellow drawing-room,' said the Prime Minister, 'and fill him up with spiced tea and nutmeg sandwiches and other eastern delicacies so that he hasn't time to ask for the King. If he gets in here alone he'll have that dummy to bits in no time and then the fat will be in the fire, the cat will be out of the bag and the Kingdom of Astufflavia will be in the soup, all at once.'

So out they went and from then until the day of the opening of the Grand Congress they kept the Judwallah of Istapampam busier than he'd ever been in his native land.

They fed him till he nearly burst. They talked him off his feet and head over heels and inside out. They made him tell them all about Istapampam and the blue elephants and the pink bluebottles and the pampam trees that grow chutney all ready done up in bottles with corks in. And they did it all so cleverly and tactfully that the Judwallah, far from suspecting that there was anything the matter with the King, enjoyed himself so much that he was quite sorry when it was time to go to the Congress.

At length all the monarchs and potentates and princes and other magnificent and marvellous personages were assembled in the Council

Chamber for the Congress. The ministers had a bit of a job with some of them. The Emperor of Empirico would keep trying to change places with the King of Chipsi Pipsi, so that he could sit next to the Prince of Nunnymunge who was his wife's half-cousin's sister's brother and owed him fourpence. And the Nabob of Notsofast was so fat that they had to use two shoe-horns to get him into his chair.

But at last everyone was seated and the Prime Minister stood up, rang a bell, blew a whistle and waved a flag.

'Pray silence for His Majesty Watitizit, King of Astufflavia,' he cried, and at once there was silence.

Then from the throne where the dummy king with the paper face sat there came a voice.

'Welcome to Astufflavia,' it said. 'Let the Congress begin.'

And none of those beautiful and ornamental monarchs guessed for a moment that the voice was the voice of the royal housekeeper's husband who was hidden behind the throne.

Neither did they guess that the royal hand that waved so majestically was really an umbrella tied up in an old curtain with a spare glove on the end.

'Well, so far so jolly well good, my hearties,' said the Prime Minister who used to be in the navy, at the end of the first day of the Congress. 'Old King Paper Face brought that off all right.'

'Almost makes you wish he was alive,' said the Minister of Education.

And that was what caused all the trouble. Just as he said the words 'wish he was alive,' who must flit past outside the window but a fairy.

'Bless my wings,' she cried, when she heard the minister's words, 'here's someone wishing someone was alive. I'll bring them to life, that's what I'll do. And then everyone will be happy.'

So she waved her wand and worked a spell and flew merrily away, little dreaming what an awful thing she had done.

The next day the Congress was just getting ready to start and the Nabob of Notsofast was nearly wedged into his chair when the dummy, paper-faced king on the throne suddenly stood up and said in a very thin papery sort of voice:

'Four shirts, six collars, two pairs of pyjamas . . .'

The Congress was horror-struck. Several of the monarchs opened their mouths so wide they couldn't shut them again by themselves. The Nabob of Notsofast shot out of his chair with a loud pop and the Judwallah of Istapampam went purple and green in stripes and started to swear most dreadfully in Istapampamian, which happily nobody else understood.

'One pair of sheets, two vests,' went on the papery voice of the dummy king, while the Prime Minister hurriedly crossed his fingers.

'Oh, my goodness,' he groaned. 'Old Paper Face has come to life.'

'I painted his face on the back of a sheet from the laundry book,' whispered the Minister of Education, 'and he keeps on shouting out the items. We must stop him before he gets to the Queen's nightdresses at all costs.'

And they made a dash at the dummy. But King Paper Face was too quick for them. With a funny jerky unsteady sort of run, because his rolling-pin leg was shorter than the leg made of the garden rake, he was out of the Council Chamber and stumping down the passage, with the ministers and all the Congress in pursuit, the Judwallah of Istapampam waving a club that he had taken from a concealed pocket in his robes.

'Treachery, plots, mischief, the King has gone mad,' he was yelling, still talking Istapampamian in his excitement.

Down the corridor went King Paper Face, his crown falling off and revealing the scraggy head of the mop, round the corner and up the next corridor, into this door and out of that with the Congress still after him for all they were worth, which was a good deal as they were all rich. And all the time as he stumped along the thin papery voice kept on, 'Four shirts, six collars, two pairs of pyjamas,' for by this time he had come to the end of the list and was starting all over again.

'Catch him, someone,' cried the Prime Minister, who had now uncrossed his fingers again so that he could run more quickly.

Round and round the corridors they went till the Palace echoed with the shouts of 'Hold him,' 'Trip him up,' 'Hit him on the head with a poker,' and above it all rang out the monotonous papery voice, 'One pair of sheets, two vests, one pair of bed-socks.'

The boots had long since come off King Paper Face's dummy legs, and the garden rake caught in one of the rugs, pulling it after him, and jerking it from under the feet of the ministers and monarchs so that they fell in an elaborate and ornamental heap, kicking and struggling and getting all tangled up.

'Ten handkerchiefs, five towels, one table-cloth,' said the dummy king, kicking the rug off his rake foot without looking back.

The Congress sorted itself out and dashed on again.

'Whatever can all the noise and shouting be about?' asked King Watitizit, sitting up in bed and looking at the Queen as if it was her fault. 'I fear there is trouble afoot. The Judwallah may be attempting treachery.' And in spite of the Queen's efforts to stop him, His Majesty got up, put on an old set of robes that happened

to be exactly like those the dummy king was wearing, drew on a pair of riding-boots and ran very shakily into the passage.

And what with his hair being all over the place as it always is when you've just got out of bed, and his face being very white and paper-looking because he wasn't well, King Watitizit looked exactly like the dummy. In fact he looked more like a dummy than the real dummy did.

As he opened the door of his room Paper Face shot by, crying, 'Four shirts, six collars.'

'Good gracious,' exclaimed the King, who knew nothing about the ministers' make-believe king.

The next minute the whole Congress of monarchs and ministers, with the Judwallah at their head, came charging round the corner, and seeing the King they let off a yell louder than ever.

'Seize him,' came the shouts, and the Jud-wallah brought his club down whack on the King's head just where his big measle bump had been.

'Ow,' cried the King and fell flat on the floor. Then from behind came a familiar stumping sound.

'One pair of sheets, two vests,' came the voice

of Paper Face as he came clattering up the corridor smack into the arms of the monarchs. He had run right round the Palace and caught up with the people who had been chasing him.

'Why, there's two of them,' cried the Judwallah, 'by my elephant's eyebrows there is mischief afoot, I vow.' But the Prime Minister and the other ministers took no notice of him. They just flung themselves on Old Paper Face and burst the string that held him together.

'One pair of bed-so—' said the voice and stopped short in the middle of a word. The next minute there was nothing left of the make-believe king but mops and umbrellas and rakes and things and some robes and a bit of painted laundry-list; while everyone crowded round wondering whatever it was all about.

Just then the Queen put her head out of the King's room, and the monarchs and ministers had to pull themselves together and bow politely.

'Now, now, what's all this about?' she said sharply, and they all hung their heads and looked very ashamed of themselves while the King got up and they all went into the Council Chamber to sort things out.

★ ★ ★

'Gentlemen,' said the Judwallah of Istapam-pam when the PrimeMinister had explained all about the dummy king and the real King's measles, 'this was all done so that we should not be put to trouble by the Congress being put off. We owe Astufflavia an apology and I suggest that we wait until the King is quite recovered both from the measles and the unfortunate blow which I struck him, and continue the Congress later on. In the meantime if Her Majesty permits I am sure we should all love to stay here and look round Astufflavia.'

'Delighted, I'm sure,' said the Queen who was glad to see things turn out so well.

And everyone cheered while King Watitizit of Astufflavia and the Judwallah of Istapampam shook hands, thereby sealing the friendship of two powerful states which had been almost on the verge of war.

But nobody ever knew how the paper-faced king came to life.

6

The King Must Be Obeyed

'How many o's are there in salute?' asked the King of Grampustania, scratching the side of his ear with the end of his pen.

'Don't you know?' said the Queen, who didn't know either, but wasn't going to say so.

'Yes, yes, of course I know,' said the King testily, scratching his ear a bit more definitely than he meant to. 'Of course I know a little thing like that, only I've forgotten.'

'Then if you've forgotten, you don't know,' said the Queen, who had a pimple on her elbow, and felt irritating.

'Oh, really, Maggie,' protested the King, 'I do think you might try to help. Here's this Oriental Nabob person coming tomorrow, and I've got orders to send to the Admiral of the Grand Fleet and more orders to send to the Commander-in-Chief of the Grampustanian Guards. All this State business is being held up because you don't know how many o's there are in salute.' He flung down his pen, which bounced into the waste-paper basket, and took down a dictionary to look up salute, and found, of course, that it had no o's in it at all.

'There now,' said His Majesty, searching about for his pen, 'no wonder I couldn't remember how many there were when there aren't any.'

'If you really want some help, Percy,' said the Queen, 'I'll write the envelopes for those orders for you, I really will, there now.' And picking up the only inkpot on the Imperial writing-table, she went across to curl up in her favourite armchair by the fire while she wrote the envelopes, and the King, who still hadn't found his pen because the Queen had discovered it in the waste-paper basket without saying anything, had to ring for a footman to go out and buy a pen and a bottle of ink so that he could get his orders done.

At last, after the Queen had interrupted five times, three times to know whether one called an Admiral 'Esquire' and twice to ask wasn't she his nice helpful Queenie, and the Butler had interrupted once with glasses of hot milk for them both and the Queen's kitten had interrupted about fifteen times by getting himself chased through the room by the King's dog, the orders were written out, one to the Admiral, saying:

'Take flagship and meet Oriental Nabob's ship tomorrow, fire salute of twenty-four guns and conduct Nabob ashore.'

The other was to the General commanding the Grampustanian Guards, saying:

'Form guard of honour with the Grampustanian Guards at main entrance to Palace for Oriental Nabob tomorrow.'

'Thank you, my dear,' said the King, taking the envelopes from the Queen. Then he folded the orders and put them in the envelopes and sent two heralds off to deliver them.

'Well, well, that's that!' said His Majesty, rubbing his hands. But if he had only known that it wasn't that at all, but something quite different, he would have torn all his hair out instead of rubbing his hands, for he had been so bothered about with interruptions and trying to find if there were o's in salute which there aren't, that he had gone and put the Admiral's orders in the General's envelope, and the General's orders in the Admiral's envelope!

The King's Herald strode into the cabin of the Admiral of the Grand Fleet of Grampustania, feeling ever so nautical after being rowed out to the flagship in a little boat. He hitched up his trousers as he'd seen sailors do and danced a couple of steps of the Grampustanian hornpipe. But it was all wasted for the Admiral was washing himself and had his face in a basin of water so didn't see him. But as he was a positively fierce Admiral, perhaps it was just as well for the Herald he didn't see him.

'Pwou-ff,' said the Admiral, taking his face out of the basin and puffing spare drops of water all over the place. 'What is it?'

'Orders, sir; aye, aye, sir,' said the Herald, and handing the envelope to the Admiral he hitched his trousers up again and went back, trailing his hand over the side of the boat all the way.

Now some Admirals if they had been given an order to form a guard of honour with soldiers would either have thought it was a joke and taken no notice or else have guessed it was a mistake and asked some questions. But in Grampustania orders were absolutely orders and never mind why.

'Most strange,' said the Admiral, reading the orders through again. He scratched his head, then looking up his eye caught a motto nailed on the wall of his cabin: 'Ours not to reason why, ours but to do or die.' The Admiral had copied it from a book. 'The King must be obeyed,' he cried, as his eye caught it. He sprang to attention, naval fashion, whatever that is, saluted a picture of the King on another wall, kissed the flag of Grampustania on another wall and went up on deck intending most certainly to do, but hoping ever so much that he wouldn't die.

Into the guard-room of the Grampustanian Guards marched the same Herald. He clicked his heels and saluted, gave the envelope to the General, clicked his heels again, saluted again, about turned and marched out, smack into the Assistant General who was just coming in, but fortunately they used to go to school together when they were little, so no harm was done.

'Good gracious!' exclaimed the General when he read in his orders that he was to take flagships and fire salutes and naval things like that. But he too was a bit of a one for obeying orders and no questions asked. He too glanced at the motto on his wall, which he had copied from the one on the Admiral's wall one day when he went to tea with him. 'The King must be obeyed,' he cried. Then he clicked his heels, ever so much more clickily than the Herald because he had had more practice, and muttering the first bars of the Grampustanian National Anthem under his breath, he went out to obey the unlikely and unexpected commands of the King.

Next day the Queen had everyone in the Palace ready for the arrival of the Oriental Nabob simply hours too soon, partly because she always kept all the clocks fast as she liked to know that she had more time than she thought, and partly because the Nabob was so frightfully important. And of course the more important people are, the earlier one gets ready for their arrival; nobody knows why but there it is.

But whatever sorts of bother the King and Queen had had getting ready for the Nabob they were absolutely less than nothing compared with the positively ding-dong, hall-marked, genuine and absolutely outside kinds of bother the Admiral was having with the soldiers and the General with the sailors.

To begin with the General came aboard the flagship on his horse, and as horses are deliberately unsuitable on battleships that was bad enough. Then he started to drill the sailors with army drill which very few of them understood and none of them even tried to do properly. At last he got them all in a long line and gave the order 'Quick march', forgetting he wasn't on a

whopping big parade ground but on a ship, and
before he could stop them every one of those
sailors had quick-marched over the side, splosh
splash, into the sea where they splashed about
trying to keep in line but not getting anywhere
near succeeding.

And while they were all in the water, the
look-out on the mast sighted the Nabob's ship.
He recognized it at once because it looked more
like almost anything else but a ship and chiefly

like a cinema or a most exaggerated birthday cake. He shouted down to the General, but the General wasn't used to being shouted at.

'Come down here and deliver your message properly,' he called back, so the look-out man had to slide whizz down the mast, which wore his trousers out very slightly, only as they were already worn out rather exceedingly that finished them off and they came in holes.

'Nabob's ship on port bow, sir,' said the sailor, saluting.

'Why don't you click your heels?' said the General, but of course the sailor couldn't because he had no shoes or socks on. Sailors never do if they can help it, and his little pink bare heels wouldn't click. You couldn't expect them to.

The General was just going to shout an order when he thought he could do it better if he got off his horse first. But he very soon found he couldn't do it at all that way, because the horse was standing near the side of the ship and the General got off him on that side and went splash into the sea among the sailors, while the man at the wheel of the flagship, not having any orders, just put his helm over hard-a-anything-he-could-think-of and went round in circles. Then the man at the engines shot up on deck thinking a shipwreck was happening and dived overboard too.

By the time the General, who couldn't swim much unless he had one foot on the bottom, had got himself rescued and everyone else back on the ship again, it was time for the twenty-four guns but the General was so flurried and wet and anxious to do everything right that he did it wrong, and all the guns went off together instead of one at a time and nearly sank the flagship.

And worst of all, only some of the guns were supposed to be fired for the salute. The others had real shells in them ready in case of war, and two gold pinnacles and a large piece of what looked like marzipan icing were knocked off the Nabob's ship. It was easily the best shot the Grampustanian Navy had ever made, probably because they didn't mean it.

'Wa wa wa woggle a wa wa pompom wom-wom bombom yow,' came Oriental shouts from the Nabob's ship and Oriental sailors began going up and down on the deck all frenzied.

'My goodness,' gasped the General, but he had no time to gasp any more because just then he was seasick.

Goodness knows what would have been the end of it all, only happily some other battleships

81

happened to be about and they came up and managed to get the Nabob landed.

In the Palace the King, who had been walking about and sitting down by turns, jumped a yard in the air when he heard all the twenty-four guns go off at once.

'Great Grampustanian Grandmothers!' he exclaimed, 'whatever is that?'

'Motor-bus backfiring, I expect,' said the Queen, powdering her nose for the eighty-somethingth time. But the King dashed to the window, and fell back in dismay on top of the Queen who had dashed up behind him to look over his shoulder.

'Oh, oh, oh, oh!' shouted His Majesty when he had got himself sorted out, 'but this is awful. Those orders I sent. Either someone has been funny with them, or there are mutinies and things happening. Look!'

Down the drive leading to the main entrance of the Palace was supposed to be drawn up the Guard of Honour for the Nabob. But gracious, it had been drawn too much up. All the soldiers were up in the trees with boots off. The Admiral was no more used to drilling soldiers than the General was to drilling sailors and he sent them all up aloft like sailors.

'We must stop it, stop it at once,' cried His Majesty, distractedly. 'Quick, quick, get in some heralds and send them out with some orders. Fetch someone and tell them something. Where's my State sword? Oh dear, tut tut.'

But there was no time to do anything, and no time to fetch anyone, for just then, with a most terrific din of assorted Oriental supposed-to-be-music, along came the Nabob seated on a green elephant – it was an ordinary grey one, but he'd had it painted so as to be unusual – and accompanied by dancing-girls, fortune-tellers, flower-strewers, road-sweepers, head cooks and bottlewashers, to say nothing of factotums, teetotums, whatsanames, thingummybobs, hodyecallems and gadgetty-pushers. He was also accompanied by one small boy who had got away from his mother and was trying to give a bun to the green elephant.

'Your Excellency,' said the King when the Nabob was ushered into his presence. 'Oh, how can I express my regrets at this most inexcusable – er-er-er—'

'Mess-up,' said the Queen.

'Shush,' said the King, nudging her so that she had to powder her nose again.

'This-er-er – I mean soldiers up trees and all that. Really, Excellency, some unfriendly agency I fear has been at work to – to – er – to – to—'

'Three, four, five,' said the Queen, but at that moment in came the General, still sopping wet, and the Admiral still quite dry, of course. They saluted and handed the King the orders he had sent them with 'Done' written in one corner.

The King looked at them a few times each, then with a hoarse cry he staggered to his feet.

'Gracious, O most Excellent Excellencies,' he cried, 'it has all been my own fault. Alas, and woe is me.'

'Er – might I ask what has been Your Majesty's own fault?' asked the Nabob, speaking the King's language most beautifully because he was learned.

'Oh dear, oh dear,' groaned the King, 'those soldiers up trees, and whatever must have happened on the flagship and about the salute of guns. Oh, oh.'

'Oh, all that,' said the Nabob, smiling and showing ever so many more teeth than you would expect anyone to have. 'Well, well, I must say I thought it was going rather far shooting pieces off my ship though it does look a bit like an Aunt Sally, but my people like it you know, just as they like to see me on a green elephant. It gets rather trying being Oriental at times even when you're used to it. But as to all the rest, why we had rather fun chasing your ship and why shouldn't soldiers go up trees? They were nicely out of the way of my elephant there.'

'Well, I never,' gasped the King, 'your Excellency is most nice, but surely your Excellency jokes . . .'

'I should say I do,' said the Nabob. 'Have

you heard this one?' And he at once proceeded to tell the King and Queen no end of such catastrophically funny stories that very soon both of them were absolutely rolling on the throne with laughter and the Queen's robes split up the back four times and had to be secretly sewn up again on her.

'Well, it's a remarkably fortunate thing for us that the Nabob turned out to be such a jolly sort of person,' said the King afterwards. 'But, for goodness' sake, Maggie, next time I have orders to send out don't you go writing the envelopes. I shouldn't have mixed them up if you'd let me alone.'

'Oh, that's right,' said the Queen, 'blame me for it all, just because I tried to help.' And she began to cry.

'There, there,' said the King, 'I didn't mean it,' and they kissed and made it up, but the Queen's idea of making it up included an enormous box of chocolates, three new hats, a bottle of perfume, and two visits to the pictures in the most expensive seats.

7

The Secret of Squelchways

The Fifteenth Duke of Squelchways sat with the Duchess in Squelchways Castle, staring at rows of paintings of bygone Dukes of Squelchways. And the more they looked at them the more they didn't like them.

'Of course,' said the Duke, 'whoever painted them may not have been as clever as he thought he was. That might account for them looking so – er – drastic.'

'And the frames need dusting,' said the Duchess. 'They always do.'

'They're worth a lot of money,' murmured the Duke, who could hardly remember what a lot of money was like as it was so long since they'd had any. 'And we certainly need a lot of money to repair the castle or it will absolutely fall jolly well down.'

'Then why don't we sell them?' said the Duchess, getting out of her chair five-eighths of a second before a portion of ceiling fell into it.

'My dear' protested the Duke, 'one can't sell

the family portraits. It simply isn't done. Besides nobody will buy them. I've already tried.'

But worse than the Squelchways family paintings – oh, a lot worse – was the bust of the First-of-all Duke of Squelchways which sometimes stood in a dark corner of the hall, sometimes in a not-much-used room and sometimes in other places. But wherever it stood nobody could stand it. It was awful.

'Nobody can say the Squelchways haven't improved in looks,' said the Duke, glancing from the portraits to the bust, and then to his own reflection in a mirror.

'Nobody need say it,' retorted the Duchess. 'It's one of those things that can be seen at a glance.'

'Yes, my dear,' said the Duke, not feeling quite sure whether this was polite or not. 'Now let's have another go at solving the family secret.'

The family secret consisted of a very cross-word-puzzle sort of conundrum that was engraved on the base of the bust of the First Duke of Squelchways. The Fifteenth Duke had copied it out on paper so that they didn't have to keep looking at the bust, which nobody could bear to do. This was the inscription:

You have only to do what you feel most inclined,
And it's perfectly certain you'll very soon find
That riches beyond all your wildest of dreams
Will be yours, for a thing may not be what it seems.

'Stupid,' said the Duchess.

'Well, you know,' said the Duke, 'it was probably all right in his day, because doing what you felt most inclined would more than likely mean going out with armies and collaring someone else's lands. Then if their place was better than yours, although it didn't look it, there you were.'

'And a lot of good that does us,' said the Duchess. 'The only time you ever tried collaring something of someone else's was when you were little and went with young Baron Oopsala into Farmer Plownow's orchard. And instead of riches you got a tummy-ache because things weren't what they seemed as far as the apples being ripe was concerned.'

'I believe doing what you feel inclined may have something to do with the bust itself,' said the Duke.

'If I did what I felt inclined with it I'd give it away,' said the Duchess.

'That wouldn't bring riches beyond our wildest dreams,' said the Duke.

'It would save plenty of dusting and a lot of trouble with the housemaids,' put in the Duchess. 'Anyway, there's a Bazaar on Saturday at the Town Hall and I vote we send old funny face along as our contribution. It will save us buying something to send.'

'Good idea,' said the Duke, 'and I'll see if I can get a nice fat prize offered for the ugliest thing in the Bazaar. We'd be sure to win it with that.'

But things didn't turn out quite as they expected. For one thing, somebody else had sent a crochet thingummy-whatsname which looked much worse than the bust because there was more of it, and won the prize easily. For another thing, as the Duke had suggested the prize, he had to give it, which hadn't been his idea at all. And worst of all someone bought the bust and sent it to the Duke and Duchess as a present.

'I shall take it out and lose it,' said the Duchess.

She dropped it over a bridge into the river, but a boat was going by underneath and it fell into the Captain's dinner. That caused so much trouble they had to ask the Captain to tea to smooth him down and of course he brought the bust back.

The Duke took it out and left it in a bus, but it came back through the Lost Property Office and they had to pay a reward.

They changed it for a fairly fancy fern with a hawker sort of man in the street. But he took it round to the side door and sold it back to the second housemaid, who put it back in its place hoping no one had missed it.

They posted it without any stamps and addressed it nowhere.

But the Post Office sent it back with some-thing-and-whatpence to pay.

'This is dreadful,' groaned the Duke. 'Doing what you like with the bust seems to cost no end of riches instead of bringing them.'

'We must be doing the wrong thing,' said the Duchess. 'Perhaps we shouldn't do it ourselves. You know what I mean. Perhaps getting rid of family busts is one of those isn't-done things, like selling the family portraits, or shooting foxes. Perhaps we ought to get someone else to do it for us.'

'Pah,' snorted the Duke. But as he thought it didn't sound such a bad idea, they went along to see the Cook.

'We thought you might like to send this to one of your friends as a little present,' said the Duchess.

'You're very kind, mum, I mean, Your Grace,' said the Cook, thinking it was a bit unfair to push the thing off on her like that. But she couldn't say so. When the Duke and Duchess had gone, she thought again. And this time she thought she wouldn't mind getting rid of the bust herself because she couldn't bear the sight of it. And she had a cousin who had once sent her some chocolates made of soap for a lark, and she thought that this might be a good sort of return lark, as you might say.

Next day the Grand Countess of Gadzooks came to tea. She looked about three hundred years old, drove up in a purple and yellow coach drawn by spotted horses and had a terrific appetite for lemon-cheese tarts.

'It's good to see someone values family portraits in these days,' she said, looking at the pictures of the bygone Squelchways on the wall, 'even though yours are an ugly lot. Give me another cup of tea and tell me about the neighbours, Hetty,' she said to the Duchess. 'Not using the tea-service I gave you, I see. Put in the attic because you couldn't stand it, I suppose. Not that I blame you, I couldn't stand it myself. That was why I gave it to you. Aren't there any more lemon-cheese tarts?'

The Duke and Duchess were trying to think what to say in answer to all this, because the Countess's conversation rather took your breath away. Then she went on again.

'I came across something about Squelchways the other day that might interest you, though it's probably all nonsense,' she said, half-way through her fourth tart. 'Young Hector was rummaging about in the library. You remember Hector, of course, Carrie Carraweigh's second boy. All freckles and ginger hair. Has trouble with his tonsils. But there, you wouldn't know about that. He'd dragged out the biggest book he could find, and it turned out to be legends of old family castles. Of course, the boy simply hooted with delight because apparently most of the legends were about secret passages and that sort of thing. Most unhealthy they must have been, I always think. I mean they couldn't have been swept out much. I hope you make your housemaids sweep thoroughly, Hetty. Germs, you know. There's more danger in a handful of dust than a cage full of tigers in my opinion. I'll have another tart if you've got one. You probably think I'm an old glutton over these things, but they're about the only pleasure I can indulge in nowadays. Where was I?'

'You were telling us about the book of legends,' said the Duke, carefully going back to what seemed to be the place where the news had left off and the talk on housekeeping begun.

'Yes, legends of old castles. Of course I thought of you, and when Hector had gone I had a look myself to see if Squelchways was mentioned.'

'And was it?' asked the Duchess, saying something quickly while she could think of something to say and see a chance of saying it both at once.

'Oh yes, some nonsense about the First Duke making off with some diamonds he found in a brigand's cave. Too impossible, my dears. And as if that wasn't enough, there was some fairy-tale about the Duke having a plaster bust of himself made, with the diamonds inside it for safety. Where the people who make up these legends get their ideas from I can't think. I thought you'd like to know about it especially as you've got a bust of the old Duke. An abominable-looking thing if I remember, but I shouldn't take any notice of the story if I were you. It's probably a pack of nonsense like most of these old tales.'

The Duke and Duchess said nothing, but they were thinking so furiously you could almost hear their brains whizzing round. Diamonds! And hidden in the old Duke's bust! If the legend was true, it was the answer to the secret of Squelchways! And why shouldn't it be true? Didn't the inscription on the bust say something about wealth beyond wildest dreams? And something about a thing not being what it seemed. Mightn't that not mean that the bust wasn't what it seemed but really a hiding-place for the diamonds? And they'd given it to the Cook to give away!

'We daren't say anything about it to the Countess,' thought the Duke. 'She's such a one for preserving old family portraits she'd be horrified if she knew we'd given away the old family bust.'

So the old Countess went on talking and eating tarts while the Duke and Duchess went on saying nothing but feeling as if they would go off bang any moment. And the precious bust of the old Duke was all too probably at that moment miles and miles away!

At last the castle ran out of lemon-cheese tarts. The Countess took three pink indigestion tablets, kissed the Duke and Duchess imperiously on their foreheads, and the purple and yellow coach drove off with the spotted horses jingling their harness like a fire engine.

Before the beat of the hoofs and rumble of the wheels had even begun to fade in the distance the Duke and the Duchess were in the kitchen talking so rapidly to the Cook that she let three lots of milk boil over and trod in the cat's dinner.

'I'm sure I'm awfully sorry, mum, I mean, Your Grace,' she spluttered, 'but the fact is, that is to say I . . .'

'Who did you give it to? Where did you send it? Where has it gone?' gabbled the Duke and Duchess.

'Well, you see, I – er – I, that is, it slipped out of my hand like and it – er . . .' stammered the Cook.

'Smashed to bits?' squealed the Duke and Duchess.

'Yes, Your Grace,' said the Cook, calming down now that the worst was over, 'but I didn't think it mattered so much seeing as you wanted to get rid of it, Your Grace, and one way being as good as another, so I thought.'

'Where are the pieces?' hissed the Duke.

'I threw them in the dustbin,' said the Cook.

'What?' shrieked the Duchess.

'I wrapped them up in paper so that the dustman shouldn't cut himself on the edges,' said the Cook.

The Duke shot off to the dustbin and nearly fell inside in his excitement. It was empty except for disinfectant-smelling mauve powder.

'The dustmen have been not an hour ago, Your Grace,' said the Cook.

The Duke bounced off and clambered on to the only horse in the place, which was the one used to pull the garden roller. He urged it on to catch up with the dustmen, but it was so used to pulling nothing but a garden roller that it wouldn't go fast. Then when at last it did gallop, the Duke who hadn't ridden for ages fell off, once in a bush, and twice in a puddle, before at last he caught up with the dustmen.

Thank goodness they hadn't opened the paper bundle. There it was on top of the cart. The Duke recognized the paper. It was what the laundry had sent back the wrong shirt in. He gave the dustmen a shilling each and galloped off clutching the precious packet, leaving the dustmen clutching their heads and wondering what was what.

'Got it back, puff puff, thank goodness,' he panted as he dashed into the castle.

The Duchess snatched the packet from him. He snatched it back again. The paper burst open and out fell six ham sandwiches and a bun!

Down in the kitchen the Cook's little boy was saying:

'Mummy, look what you gave me instead of

my lunch. It was a heap of bits of broken china-looking stuff and a lot of dirty marbles.'

'I . . .' began the Cook. Then the Duke and Duchess burst in again, but no milk boiled over this time because Cook hadn't had time to put any on.

'The old Duke's bust,' cried the Duke.

'He certainly has,' said the Duchess.

They grabbed up the heap of bits.

'Oh, it's a sell after all,' wailed the Duchess. 'Nothing but a lot of silly marbles. If ever there were any diamonds someone has had them.'

'No! No! No!' shrieked the Duke, 'these aren't marbles, they're diamonds all right.

Diamonds in the rough, my dear. They don't sparkle till they're cut and polished.' Goodness knows how he knew. He must have read it in an encyclo-whatsname. The secret of Squelchways was solved. So was the problem of how to get rid of the ugly bust of the first Duke.

'What beats me,' said the Duchess, 'is why we never spotted what the inscription meant. "You have only to do what you feel most inclined." I felt most inclined to smash the nasty-looking thing to bits, but I never thought of doing it.'

'Ha, ha, yes,' said the Duke, 'of course, that's what the old Duke must have meant. He evidently knew nobody would be able to stand the look of the thing. Probably he made it himself and hid the diamonds in it. Then he carved that puzzle sort of inscription. Of course, anyone who did what they felt inclined and smashed the wretched thing would soon have found wealth beyond their wildest dreams, just as we have.'

'Well,' said the Duchess, 'I think the least we can do is to send the Countess a case of about a hundred lemon-cheese tarts for telling us about the legend, and the Cook's boy a double-sized lunch to make up for the one he missed.'

8

The Unsuitable Suits

There was to be a highly important and drastically dignified kind of function at the Royal Palace of Taradidledovia, for no less a person than His Decorative Flamboyance Prince Rococo of Okokoko was to visit the kingdom.

'I must order a new Court suit,' said the Baron Bothwaze; 'this one is most last-year's looking.'

'So must I,' said Count Bakwerdz who had really only just had a new one, but he wasn't going to be outdone by the Baron.

'Me, too,' put in the Earl of Lateleigh and Sir Samuel Somewatt.

So they all went arm-in-arm along to the establishment of Ferdinand Fitzluvly, the Court Tailor, and spread themselves across the pavement so much that they swept up the Honourable Onniswar Malliparnce and the Marquis of Mennilotz who didn't want new Court suits at all, and shuzzled them along too.

'Good morning, Your Excellent Gracious Honourable Lordship Gentlemen,' said the Tailor, rubbing his hands and doing his best to get all their titles in at once.

Then there began a most fast and furious measuring up of arms and legs and shouting out of rum-sounding words by Mr Fitzluvly to his assistant tailors.

'Oh, ha, ha, ha, he, he, he-e-e-e-e,' giggled Baron Bothwaze, squirming about all ways at once because he was terribly ticklish and couldn't stand being measured much.

'Don't make it too tight,' reminded Count Bakwerdz, who always looked forward to making his suits last a long time and didn't want to grow out of them.

The Earl of Lateleigh said nothing at all because he had his mouth rather full of some nougat his aunt had given him. Sir Samuel Somewatt and the Honourable Onniswar Malliparnce had a somewhat twisted-up sort of argument about how fast they could go on their bicycles, while the Marquis of Mennilotz, who already had fifteen Court suits but didn't mind if he had some more, just went to sleep and had to be rolled about and folded up and twiddled round simply tremendously to get all his measurements, of which there were many lots because he was fattish.

At last Mr Fitzluvly had done all his measuring and bowed the six noble gentlemen out at the door, tripping over the mat and measuring his own length on the floor which was quite unnecessary.

Presently the six Court suits were finished and delivered in six very high-class boxes and wrapped in very select Court tissue-paper.

Baron Bothwaze tried his on and found it was much too big, both sideways and longways.

Count Bakwerdz put his on backwards by

mistake, but it was so much too large he was able to turn right way round in it without taking it off.

The Earl's suit was too large as well, so was Sir Samuel's and the Honourable Onniswar's.

'Disgraceful!' they all said when they had told each other. 'It may be excusable for a nobleman to be too big for his boots, but it simply is not done for him to be too small for his clothes.'

They went round in a batch to see the Marquis and found him with his servants who were having the most exaggerated time with shoe-horns and glove-stretchers and rubber mallets trying to squeeze, wedge, and gently tap the fattish Marquis into his Court suit which was absolutely sizes and sizes too small.

'We must take the things back to the Tailor at once,' said the Earl. 'The very idea! What can the man be thinking about?' As a matter of fact Mr Fitzluvly was at that moment thinking about a nice hot cup of cocoa and a currant cake which he was just going to have, but that had nothing to do with anything much.

The Marquis came out of his too small suit with a series of loud pops like corks coming out of bottles and felt glad he hadn't got any farther into it than he had, which would have been impossible anyway; and round they all surged to the Tailor's in rages, tempers, dudgeons high and low, dithers and dismays, according to how much the wrong size their suits were.

'But Excellent Graces and – and Most Honourable Lordshippishnesses,' stammered Mr Fitzluvly, when he had managed to understand what they were talking about, which wasn't easy because they all talked at once, and then all left off at once for each other to talk, then all began again at once, each thinking the others were waiting for him. 'But Excellencies, I cannot believe it,' he cried. 'Such a thing has never happened before.'

'It had better not happen again,' grumbled Baron Bothwaze, but the Tailor didn't hear him for he was busy getting the unsuitable suits out of the high-class boxes and select Court tissue-paper. 'Perhaps Excellencies will be kind enough to try the suits on again so that I may see what is wrong?' he said.

Oh yes, Excellencies were quite kind enough to do that. They all went into separate little screened-off sort of roomettes so as to be nice and private while they changed their clothes, in case one had a hole in his sock or a safety-pin where there should have been a button, or anything dis-noble like that; while Mr Fitzluvly waited with what patience he could, which was none at all, until they were ready.

Suddenly the Baron shot out of his little room.

'Extraordinary,' he cried, 'it fits, it fits.' And so it did. His suit was as sleek and snug and beautiful as could be.

Mr Fitzluvly was just going to rub his hands when out shot the Count, the Earl, the Honourable and Sir Samuel who had all taken exactly the same time to change, goodness knows why. And wonderfully amazing thing, their suits all fitted them perfectly.

They waited for the Marquis but he didn't shoot out of his little room because he'd gone to sleep in it. But he had his suit on. Yes, he had, and without any servants or shoe-horns or glove-stretchers or rubber mallets, and with not the least bit of squeezing or stretching or tapping on the head.

'Really, Excellencies,' said the Tailor, putting his nose in the air rather, 'I do not see that you have anything to complain of.'

And, of course, the six noblemen had to agree. Their suits fitted perfectly. They could only go back to their little rooms, change back into their ordinary things, and go home with their Court suits all wrapped up in the paper and boxes again.

'Look here, I believe there's some mischief about these suits,' said the Earl of Lateleigh on the way. 'That Tailor looks a bit wizardy to me. I vote we all go to my place and try the suits on again to make sure.'

'Righto, yes, rather,' said all the others, except the Honourable Onniswar Malliparnce, who had a hole in each sock and safety-pins where nearly all his buttons should have been.

But along to the Earl's place they went, got their suits out of the boxes and changed into them again.

'By the beard of my brother's barber,' cried Sir Samuel Somewatt, as soon as he'd got his suit on.

'Gadz-what-is-names!' yelled Count Bakwerdz.

'I knew it, I knew it!' screamed the Earl, 'worse than before.'

For goodness gracious, each of them found his suit was now ever so much too small for him, except Baron Bothwaze, and his was so big he could have got into it several times over without noticing or undoing the buttons only he didn't bother to.

'Back to the Tailor!' roared the Earl. Hurriedly they flung off the suits and flung on their own things again and were half-way to the Tailor's before they discovered the Marquis of Mennilotz had gone to sleep again and was being dragged along amongst them with far too few clothes on. Back they dashed, and got him woken up and the rest of his things on and set off again.

'Ought to be ashamed of 'self,' roared the Earl, flinging the suits at the Tailor without any boxes or tissue-paper round them.

'Call 'self tailor, pah!' exploded the Baron.

Mr Fitzluvly couldn't understand it at all. He spoke most soothingly and at last managed to entice those six annoyed noblemen into the little rooms again and persuaded them to try on the suits once more.

Tantalizing tape-measures! Every suit fitted its wearer perfectly! There was absolutely not a wrinkle or a crease or a speck out of place.

The noblemen shook their heads and scratched their heads both at once, which was difficult because they kept missing and scratching where there was no head. But there was nothing to do except to have the suits wrapped up again and take them home.

At last it was the day of the great function. His Decorative Flamboyance Prince Rococo of Okokoko had arrived with much ta-ra-ra-ra on trumpets and a great deal of drm-m-m-rm-rm-rm on drums and plenty of hurray-y-y-y from the populace.

Baron Bothwaze was just beginning to get into his Court suit, ready to go to the Palace, when Count Bakwerdz dashed in looking the most dreadful sight. His breeches were too tight, his coat was too big and his waistcoat was all over the place.

'That rascally tailor has bewitched the suits again,' he yelled.

Hurriedly the Baron climbed into his suit. It was awful! It fitted where it touched, but hardly touched anywhere. Hand-in-hand they ran round to the Earl of Lateleigh and found him in such a rage that the fire had gone out. His suit was as bad as theirs. Big here, small there, right size nowhere.

Terrible!

Round to Sir Samuel Somewatt they tore, then to the Honourable Onniswar Malliparnce.

Just the same; suits like sacks. Most un-courtlike. Hanging in folds or stretched to bursting-point. The Marquis of Mennilotz wasn't asleep for the first time they could remember because of the time he was having with all his garments too small, but some of them more too small than others.

The function was due to start in less than an hour.

'To the Tailors',' yelled the Earl, brandishing the Marquis's braces which were the only sort of weapon he could find.

'B-b-but,' stuttered the Tailor as they charged in.

'Traitor, wizard, rascal, varlet,' screamed the enraged six, shaking fists and hairbrushes and braces at him. 'Denounce him! To the stake with him! Gr-r-r.'

What a situation! The highly important function due to start so soon and six noblemen with their Court suits all in a muddle! Thank goodness the Tailor had his wits about him, although they didn't show much when he was standing still.

Somehow or other, he managed to smooth down the fizzling furious noblemen and get the unsuitable suits away from them. Carefully

he examined the suits. Carefully he looked at the noblemen. Suddenly he gave a great cry and began arranging the noblemen in a row. Then he cried: 'I have it. Now I understand.'

'Yes,' whispered the noblemen, craning forward with their eyes all goggly to hear how the strange bewitching of their suits had come about.

'Look,' said the Tailor, pointing at a mirror opposite.

They looked. And they noticed for the first time that they were a sort of graduated set. The

Baron was quite little and short. The Count wasn't quite so little or short. The Earl was a bit bigger and rather taller. Sir Samuel was larger and taller still. The Honourable Onniswar Malliparnce was quite big and the Marquis was positively fattish. They'd never stood in a row in just those positions before so they hadn't known they went up like steps, as it were.

'Well?' they asked, still not seeing much but feeling they ought to.

'Why,' cried the Tailor, biting his tape-measure in halves in his excitement. 'Don't you see, when the suits were first delivered, by some mistake you each got one too large. The Baron got the one meant for the Count, the Count had the one made for the Earl and so on. So, of course, they were all a bit too big except the one the Marquis had. He, of course, got the one the Baron should have had. No wonder it was too tiny!'

'Gracious!' exclaimed all six at once.

'Yes, indeed,' said the Tailor. 'Of course, when you brought them to me I knew whose was which but I didn't know they'd been mixed up.'

'Ha, ha,' cried the Earl suddenly, seeing a bit more. 'And when we took them the second time we each got the wrong one again because we were a bit flurried or something?'

'Exactly,' said Mr Fitzluvly.

'And,' went on the Earl a bit squeakily, thinking how clever he was, 'that time we each got the suit meant for the next smaller man.'

'Except the Baron,' said the Tailor, 'and he got the great big suit made for the Marquis. Of course the last time you evidently got all fuddled through being excited about the strangeness of the suits and the coming function, and you simply got the coats and breeches and everything positively assortedly muddled.'

They all looked at one another and burst out laughing.

'Oh, I say, we really apologize, you know,' said the Earl, 'for calling you those names, I mean.'

'Not at all,' said the Tailor, and they were just beginning to be all polite with each other when the Palace clock chimed the hour. The function was just commencing! The Tailor called in his assistants. The noblemen dashed into their little rooms. Arms and legs and breeches and socks with holes in flew about all over the place, and almost before the booming notes of the clock had died away those six noble gentlemen came more or less calmly out of the Tailor's each dressed beautifully in his perfectly fitting Court suit and set out for the Palace.

The function was a great success. The six noblemen enjoyed themselves immensely. Especially the Marquis of Mennilotz who fell asleep immediately after he had been presented to the Prince, and only woke up just in time for the refreshments.

9

The Dragon Who Cheated

The Kingdom of Urgburg-under-Ug was as pleasant a little place as you could wish to find. In fact, it was a great deal more pleasant than most people would dream of wishing to find. It was beautiful sunshiny summer all the year except on the 15th March when there was always a slight snowstorm.

But owing to a special arrangement that had something to do with leap years and that kind of thing, the 15th March occurred only twice in ten years in Urgburg-under-Ug.

Then again, the King and Queen of Urgburg-under-Ug were two exceedingly charming people, and about the only law that was ever enforced in the kingdom was one which said that no one was to be unhappy.

There was a special force of joyous policemen employed particularly to see that this law was not disobeyed. If anyone fell over and hurt himself, or dropped down a grating a penny that he was going to buy sweets with or anything

115

like that, these joyous policemen would make funny faces and give them new pennies which the King secretly provided himself. That will just show you how nice it was in the Kingdom of Urgburg.

There were only two things wrong with the Kingdom of Urgburg-under-Ug.

One of them was its name which was slightly difficult to say and definitely difficult to spell, but that didn't matter very much because nobody minded whether it was pronounced properly or not except the Urgburg Broadcasting Company, and they knew how to pronounce it.

But there was a dragon in Urgburg, and a very unpleasant dragon at that. It arrived quite suddenly from goodness knows where and started stamping on places and burning things up with its fiery breath, and kicking things down with its spiky feet.

'This dragon business is most distressing,' said the King, who had gathered all his ministers together to discuss what should be done. 'What can we do to release the kingdom from such a monster?'

'Perfectly simple, my dear Gilbert,' said the Queen, who wasn't supposed to be at the conference at all. 'All you have to do is to issue a proclamation and say that you offer half the kingdom and the hand of the Princess in marriage to whoever shall slay the dragon.'

'But, my dear Agnes,' protested the King, 'you know perfectly well we haven't a princess.'

'Neither we have,' said the Queen; 'I was forgetting.'

She put her thumb in her mouth because it helped her to think, then remembering there was company present, if you can count ministers and chancellors as company, she hurriedly took it out again, and said, 'Well, we can still offer half the kingdom and there'd be sure to be plenty of nice strong dragon-slaying sort of people who would be willing to do a spot of work for a prize like that.'

'That's right enough,' said the King; 'they might even be more willing to slay the dragon for half the kingdom alone than if they thought they had to marry a princess as well. I don't suppose all dragon-slaying people are very used to princesses, and it might put them out a bit. You know what I mean – having to turn half a kingdom into a little kingdom of its own and be majestic sort of majesties themselves, so that the Princess should not feel homesick.'

'That's what I think,' put in the Prime

Minister. 'I know a man who has a sister who used to know a friend who once heard of a dragon-slaying sort of man who slew a dragon to win half a kingdom and a princess, and he used to say—'

'Now never mind what he used to say,' broke in the Queen hurriedly, guessing that whatever it was it would take a long time to tell because she used to say things like that to her friends and it used to take her ages, 'let's think out the proclamation.'

'Certainly, my dear,' said the King, licking his pencil which was copying-ink, only he had forgotten, and it made his tongue all purple. 'Let me see, how does this sound? "Wanted, superior dragon-slayer" . . .'

'No, no,' said the Queen, 'don't say "superior". It doesn't matter what sort of a dragon-slayer he is so long as he slays the dragon.'

'Pardon me, Majesties,' put in the Lord High Marshal of Heralds, who knew all about proclamations because he used to be a herald in another kingdom before he came to Urgburg, and had shouted many a one round the streets. 'Pardon me, but if I might make so bold as to say so, proclamations ought to start with "Oyez".'

'Oyez,' said the King.

'Oh! no,' said the Queen, 'that is much too old-fashioned. We must be up-to-date.'

'Dragons are rather old-fashioned,' put in the Prime Minister who had not quite forgiven the Queen for stopping him from telling them about the man that his friend's sister's acquaintance had heard of, and thought this was a chance to get his own back. But by this time the King, who had been writing away like anything on the back of an odd piece of paper for several minutes, suddenly said, 'Listen to this. "Oyez, oyez – wanted dragon-slayer to slay dragon" – that doesn't sound quite right, but I can't think of any other way of saying it – "half kingdom reward, no princess, no questions asked".'

At this, there was a tremendous babble of voices, as everybody started talking at once and saying how they thought the proclamation ought to go, and the noise became so loud that the King had to go outside and have a cannon or two let off to get silence.

'Now, I'll tell you what we'll do,' said the Queen; 'everyone is to go away and write out in nice clear handwriting their own idea of a proclamation. Then we shall all meet again here at this time tomorrow and there'll be a small prize for the one whose proclamation is considered the best.'

Everybody applauded this idea except the King, who guessed that he would have to pay for the little present, but before he could say anything, the tea bell rang, and everybody streamed out, headed by the Queen, who was rather good at that sort of thing.

Next day, at the appointed time, the proclamations were read out.

The Lord Chancellor had written his in rhyme, because he liked to think he was rather a poet, although nobody else could bear to think it.

'Oyez, oyez, and be it known
A dragon-slayer's needed
To free the kingdom, save the throne,
So let this call be heeded.
And as reward for such as can
This monster overthrow,
One-half this land Elysian
Shall to the slayer go.'

'What does "Elysian" mean?' asked the King, who had an aunt named Elizabeth Ann, and thought it might have something to do with her and didn't want to get aunts mixed up with state affairs.

'I don't like "such as can",' said the Queen, 'and anyway, who said a proclamation had to rhyme? Next, please.'

'Oyez, oyez,' began the Prime Minister, then feeling that he had done quite well so far, he went on in a louder voice, 'slay the dragon and win a handsome prize. Half the kingdom for a successful attempt. No entrance fee, no difficulties. Their Majesties' decision is final.'

'That sounds as if a dragon was a sort of crossword puzzle,' said the Queen, who didn't hold with crossword puzzles because the King could do them better than she could. 'Next, please.'

This was the Lord High Marshal of Heralds. He popped up very quickly and in a voice that could be heard all over the place read out:

'Oyez, oyez, oyez. Whereas the Kingdom of Urgburg-under-Ug is suffering under the onslaughts of a dragon, be it known that we by our royal privilege do hereby offer half the said kingdom, together with all the appurtenances thereof, as prize or reward to whomsoever shall slay the monster. Given under our hand this so and so day.'

Of course that was by far the best attempt of any, but the King said he thought the Lord High Marshal of Heralds knew too much about proclamations.

Then the rest of them had a go at reading out their attempts except two of the ministers who had not been able to get any further than chewing the end of a pencil, and one who had been looking over the Lord Chancellor's shoulder, but hadn't been able to read his writing.

'Well,' said the Queen, rather briskly. 'I did one myself.' She read out:

'Oyez, oyez. We have had the most terrible dragon ravishing the kingdom lately, and what do you think it's been doing? I mean to say, too devastating, you know. Why, my dears, positively stamping on places and all that. Something must be done about it, so the King and myself thought that if we could get someone to slay the dragon, because we feel sure that nobody really likes the nasty thing, we would give him half the kingdom for his trouble. So—'

'Here, here,' broke in the King.

'Don't applaud until I've finished,' said the Queen, thinking he meant an applauding sort of thing like 'Hear, hear!'

'But you can't have a proclamation like that,' said the King.

Then the King and Queen started arguing, partly about the proclamation but very much more so about the small prize, chiefly because the Queen's idea of a small prize was a very big one.

'I tell you what we'll do,' said the King at last, 'you shall have a nice diamond necklace for your prize for the proclamation, but we'll use the Lord High Marshal of Heralds' proclamation because it sounds better.'

'All right,' replied the Queen, who didn't mind so long as she got the prize, and as nobody else minded either because the King promised them all consolation prizes, the matter was settled.

But although the proclamation was settled, the dragon wasn't, and next day news came that he had kicked down two more castles.

The dragon sat at the mouth of his cave cleaning his claws with a tree-trunk.

'Huh! Huh!' he growled, 'so they want to get me killed, do they? I'll teach them to send out proclamations. I'll teach them a thing or two about killing dragons.'

He had heard the proclamation read out because he had rather good ears and four of them at that, two on each of his two heads.

'Disgraceful, I call it,' said one head.

'I've got an idea,' said the other.

'Well, out with it,' said the first.

'Psp, psp,' said the other, trying to whisper.

'What say?' said the first head.

'Get suit of armour, disguise self as champion, pretend kill own self, claim half kingdom as reward.'

'Good idea, but don't talk like telegram,' said the first head, talking like one itself.

The dragon shook one head and nodded the other, and went round to one of the castles he had kicked down and rummaged about to find some armour. He had a very severe portion of trouble getting himself into the armour, partly because his tail was rather long and he had to wind it round himself which made him rather fat, and partly because he had to get both his heads into one helmet.

'They say two heads are better than one,' said the first head.

'I can't see it myself,' said the second.

'Move over a bit,' said the first.

At last the dragon got himself all fastened

up by using about four-and-a-half suits of armour to cover him, and set out for the King's palace.

'Majesty,' he said, bowing before the throne as he was ushered into the King's presence, 'I come as your champion. I will kill the dragon if you promise me the reward you have offered.' He said this with both his heads at once, so it sounded nice and loud even though the visor of his helmet was down so that no one could see he was really the dragon himself.

'Ask him to open his hat,' said the Queen, who was not used to people talking through their helmets at her, although she used to say that some of the ministers talked through their hats, but that, of course, was a different thing.

'Shush,' whispered the King, 'you may upset him, and look what a nice big champion he is. No dragon will stand a chance against such a whopper.' Then aloud he said, 'Certainly go and slay the dragon, bring back proof that you have slain it and half the kingdom shall be yours.'

'Majesty,' boomed the dragon's two heads, 'it shall be done.'

And with a clatter and clang of all four-and-a-half suits of armour, he strode out of the

Palace with such a swish that all the blinds came down and three of the ministers thought it was night-time and went to bed.

Once again the dragon was sitting outside his cave, but this time he wasn't cleaning his claws. He was very carefully cutting a circular piece out of the side of a large tray. Then he put the tray on his shoulder with the cut-out piece round one of his necks, held it there with one paw, put his other head on one side, and looked at his reflection in the pond.

'Excellent,' said the first head.

'Looks just as if you are carrying the dragon's head on a tray,' said the second head.

'Entirely satisfactory,' said both heads together.

The dragon put his helmet on again, putting it on to one head only this time, and back he went to the Palace. He strode up the throne-room, making the windows rattle as he went. He held the head on which he wore the helmet slightly on one side and he kept the eyes on his other head closed, and as he held the tray on his shoulder, it looked for all the world as if he was a mighty champion bearing the head of the slain dragon on the tray.

Cheers went up as he went by.

'Hoorah for the dragon-slayer! Hail champion of Urgburg-under-Ug! The dragon is slain!'

'Majesty,' said the dragon, being careful to talk only with the head that was inside the helmet, 'I have slain the dragon. See, I bring his head as proof. I come to claim my reward of half the kingdom.'

'Lovely,' said the Queen, clapping her hands,

'what a horrid-looking dragon it was.'

'Terrible,' said the King.

And the dragon who didn't know whether he wanted to laugh because his plan was succeeding so well, or to be angry because they were saying such rude things about him, but who knew he mustn't do either until he got his reward, passed round the throne-room, pretending to show off the head on the tray.

Oh! dreadful situation, think of it! The dragon about to be given half the kingdom for slaying himself! Not that it would have mattered if he had slain himself, but of course he hadn't. He was tricking the King. He was tricking the entire kingdom. When he had got half the kingdom for himself he would still go on ravaging the other half. Instead of Urgburg-under-Ug being delivered from the dragon, it would be delivered to the dragon. Everything would be terrible. Oh! crafty monster! Oh! to think that nothing could be done to save the kingdom!

The King stood up.

'According to the terms of the proclamation,' he cried, 'I have much pleasure in presenting to our valiant champion one-half of the King-dom of Urgburg-under-Ug.' Then, turning to the disguised dragon, 'Won't you put the head down, sir, and take a cup of wine?'

'Oo-er,' thought the dragon, ' can't put my own head down. I'd better pretend to be a bit dashing.' Then aloud:

'Majesty, I prefer to keep the head of this monster as a trophy.'

The Queen was just going to ask what a trophy was, when from amongst the spectators a young man pushed his way forward, and ran towards the dragon.

'Go back,' cried the King, 'go away.'

But the young man didn't go back or away. He ran forward with a small bright object clasped firmly in his hand. It was a pepper-box.

He shook its contents on to the tray in front of the dragon's head.

'Arrest him,' roared the King.

The guards had taken hardly a step when—

'ATISHOO!' A most frightfully monstrous noise rang out. The head of the supposed-to-be-slain dragon had sneezed!

Pandemonium raged. The cheers that had gone up before gave place to screams of fear and howls of alarm. The King jumped up so suddenly that he kicked the throne over backwards and the Queen with it, but happily she fell on some cushions.

'He is no champion,' said the young man, pointing to the dragon who had torn the helmet off his other head and was beginning to puff out sparks, 'he is the dragon himself.'

'Huh, huh,' roared the dragon in a voice that blew all the guards' hats off in a shower. 'Yes, I am the dragon and I will have not half the kingdom but all of it. It's just my dinner-time – what a meal I'll have!' He rolled his eyes round the throne-room and blew out a jet of blue flame.

Forty-seven duchesses fainted all at once. The Lord Chamberlain climbed up on the chandelier, the Prime Minister and the Lord

Chief Justice tried to get up the chimney but got stuck half-way.

The dragon advanced, a terrifying form, upon the young man.

'Have at ye!' cried the young man, who had read in a book that champions always said that when attacking the foe. He drew his sword with a flourish. Horrors! the blade flew off the handle. Urgburg-under-Ug was undone! The last hope was gone. No, it wasn't! Marvel of all marvels! The shining sword blade flew like a streak of silver across the room and through both the dragon's heads at once, skewering them like an enormous pennyworth of cat's meat.

With a sensational crash that shook all the pictures down in the Queen's spare bedroom, the dragon fell lifeless to the floor. Serve him right for cheating. The pieces of armour from his four-and-a-half suits rolled and clanged all over the place like so many milk-churns or even more.

More cheers went up. Forty-six of the fainted duchesses came unfainted again and asked for cups of tea. The Queen climbed out of the cushions and helped the King stand the throne up again. The Lord Chamberlain dropped off the chandelier with a loud 'bong' into the middle of the floor, but didn't hurt himself much as he wore thick trousers. The Prime Minister and the Lord Chief Justice came out of the chimney followed by a large helping of soot.

The Kingdom of Urgburg-under-Ug was saved!

'But tell me,' said the King to the young man, when they were sitting down to a nice banquet to celebrate the great occasion, 'who are you and how did you guess the dragon's trick?'

'I am Prince Diddinott Dottimwun,' said the young man. 'My kingdom which is near here was stamped out of existence by the dragon the Thursday before last. I followed him and saw him preparing to trick you into giving him half your kingdom.'

'Splendid,' said the King, 'now you can have half of my kingdom, and marry the Princess, and everything will be all lovely.'

'Shush,' said the Queen, 'we haven't got a princess. You said so yourself.'

'Neither we have!' exclaimed the King, it being his turn to look rather silly.

'Never mind,' said the young man, 'everything is quite all right. I never did care much for girls, anyway.'

So the Prince ruled over half the Kingdom of Urgburg-under-Ug, but whether he cared much for girls anyway, or not, it wasn't very long before he fell in love with a rather special young duchess. So this rather unlikely sort of story comes to a nice usual sort of end because they were married and lived happily ever after.

10

The Secret Document

The Imperial Treaty of Swallowbitz, Arskmee and Meerleigh-Moorseau was a frightfully important and terribly secret sort of document. Nobody but the monarchs of those three countries was allowed to read it, and even they used to wear smoked spectacles when they read it so that they couldn't see it very clearly. That will just show you how frightfully secret it really was. There never has been such a tremendously secret kind of secret to this day, not even the secret of how the jam got into the doughnut or what happened to it when it got there because nobody finds any jam in doughnuts.

'I don't like these secret sort of documents,' said the King of Meerleigh-Moorseau, holding the treaty in both hands very tightly. 'They make me all hot and bothered.'

'Yes, Majesty,' said the Prime Minister, looking the other way in case he should catch sight of any of the words on the secret treaty.

'The trouble is,' went on the King, still

holdingontothetreatywithbothhands,'thatsecret documents like this must be hidden terribly carefully otherwise they get stolen, wars happen and thrones fall, and the price of food goes up, and goodness knows what is the end of it. But if you hide them so carefully that nobody can steal them, you are almost certain not to be able to find them yourself when they are wanted. Then if they can't be found when they are wanted, wars happen and thrones fall and the price of food goes up and goodness knows what is the end of it just the same.' He shook his head very slightly. 'It is all very puzzling and difficult. I sometimes wish I was an engine-driver or a policeman or something nice and un-noticeable instead of a king, so that wars wouldn't happen and thrones would stay where they were and the price of food would remain unaltered, and there wouldn't be anything to be an end of if I made a little mistake now and then.'

The Prime Minister looked round, being careful first of all to blindfold himself with his pocket handkerchief in case he should see any of the secret treaty. 'We have only to hide the document for two or three days,' he said, 'be-cause on Thursday afternoon, as Your Majesty knows, the Grand Conference is due, when the Swali of Swallowbitz and the Wearabowtz of Arskmee will attend, and it will be the turn of one of those Imperial Personages to take charge of the treaty.'

'Yes,' said the King mournfully. 'Unless they cheat like they did once before and toss up with a double-headed penny so that it comes to my turn again.' He placed the secret treaty on a chair and sat on it so that the Prime Minister could safely take the bandage off his eyes.

'What we have to do,' said His Majesty, 'is to find a perfectly amazing hiding-place for the treaty, somewhere where nobody will dream of looking, and wouldn't look if they did dream of it.'

'I have heard, Your Majesty,' said the Prime Minister, sitting down on another chair very carefully, partly because he was thinking so hard, and partly because he had slight pains in his back through sitting on some damp grass. 'I have heard that when you want to hide something where nobody will look for it the best thing to do is to put it in a silly sort of place where everybody can see it; like when you play "Hunt the thimble" and put the thimble on top of the clock.'

The King shook his head and was just going

to jump up when he remembered the treaty he was sitting on and stopped where he was. 'Tut, tut,' he said. 'That's all very well for thimbles, but it won't do for frightfully important secret treaties. People who go round trying to steal things like that always look in those sorts of places.'

For a few moments there was silence broken only by the ticking of the Prime Minister's watch which was a rather cheap one, and the creaking of the King's chair which was a rather weak one. Suddenly the King banged his fist on the table and spilt a lot of water out of a flower-vase on to the Queen's brand new table-centre.

'I have an idea,' he cried. 'Good gracious! and bounding buttercups! I have an idea. But what an idea! Oo-er!'

'Yes, Your Majesty?' said the Prime Minister, leaning forward eagerly.

'Listen,' said the King, getting all worked up and excited, 'but don't you say a word to anybody, or down go your wages, away goes your job, and off goes your head all at once. There is only one thing to do with the secret treaty, only one place to hide it where nobody will ever look. We are going to throw it away!'

As he said these words, the King sprang to his feet, snatched up the treaty, crumpled it into a ball and threw it into the waste-paper basket, getting it in first shot.

'Heavens!' cried the Prime Minister, jumping to his feet, and sitting down again at once because the King's astounding action had made him go all weak at the knees.

'Don't you see,' said the King, waving his hands about excitedly and causing quite a draught. 'Don't you see what a wonderful hiding-place it is! Who is going to look for a frightfully important and terribly secret document in the waste-paper basket? Nobody,' he shouted without waiting to see if the Prime Minister was going to answer. 'I tell you it is marvellous.' He flung out his hands and the Prime Minister did the same.

'Marvellous,' they both cried.

Just then in came the Queen and they immediately had to pretend they were rehearsing for charades, in case the Queen should start asking questions, which she was very likely to do, and get to know about the secret treaty which would have been frightful. Because it was so secret that even the queens of the countries concerned were not allowed to know anything about it in case they got saying things to their friends to show off.

Two days later the King and the Prime Minister came back into the room where they had put the treaty in the waste-paper basket.

'To-morrow,' said the King, 'is the Imperial Conference when I shall hand over the secret treaty to one of the other monarchs, and thank goodness for that. Now you keep watch at the keyhole, while I look in the waste-paper basket to make sure that the treaty is still there, which of course it must be.'

So the Prime Minister put his eye to the keyhole of the door, but nearly getting the key in his eye because he didn't notice it was there, while His Majesty went across to the waste-paper basket.

Suddenly there was a terrific yell from the King who leapt into the air with the waste-paper basket clutched in his hands. He turned red and then blue and then purple and then several colours which haven't got any names at all. He waved his hands about knocking things all over the place with the waste-paper basket. Then he collapsed into a chair and the chair collapsed with him.

'Majesty! Majesty!' cried the Prime Minister,

rushing across and trying to help him up but
getting all tangled up in the waste-paper basket
and the collapsed chair himself.

'Gone!' cried the King, struggling to his feet.
'The waste-paper basket is empty!'

'Gracious!' cried the Prime Minister, still
sitting on the floor, forgetting to get up in his
anxiety.

Everything was awful. The Royal dustman

had called and emptied the waste-paper baskets a day earlier than usual because it was going to be Bank Holiday the next week. The secret treaty was gone. Perhaps one of the dustmen was a spy and had done it on purpose. Or perhaps he wasn't and hadn't. Perhaps even at that moment the secret treaty was being read by all sorts of people who had no right to know that it existed. Perhaps it was even being shouted from the house-tops; there might be going to be wars. Thrones might be going to fall and the price of food might be going to go up, and certainly goodness knows what was going to be the end of it all. The King pulled himself together, so vigorously that he nearly choked himself.

'We must act at once,' he said. There is no time to be lost. We must go at once to the place where the rubbish is emptied, and search for the secret treaty. Have the horses saddled at once, call out the guards who haven't gone home for tea, and tell those who have to come back at once.'

His Majesty dashed out of the room to find the Queen.

'I am just going out to do a little rabbit-hunting, my dear,' he said, talking very casually although he felt most un-casual inside himself. He didn't dare let the Queen know anything about anything of course, because of it being so secret.

'Right-o,' said the Queen. 'Don't forget to wrap up warmly, and take your umbrella in case it rains, and I'll make you some sandwiches to take with you,' and off she ran to the kitchen where she cut the King a simply large packet of sandwiches with her own royal hands and the bread-knife.

At the royal rubbish dump three miles outside the city, the King and the Prime Minister might have been seen rummaging frenziedly among the old envelopes and torn-up bits of paper. But of course they were not seen except by the guards who were there to see that nobody else saw them.

'Any luck yet?' said the King, grabbing at a piece of paper which looked likely and then giving a terrific sneeze because it was a not-quite-empty packet of pepper which somebody had thrown away.

'Not yet,' said the Prime Minister, throwing

old cardboard boxes up in the air by the dozen as he burrowed into the heap of rubbish, 'but I may have any minute.'

'So may – atishoo – I,' said the King. He threw away the paper bag which blew across in front of the guards and set them all sneezing, and as they sneezed their armour rattled and they ran about trying to find dock leaves to put on their noses thinking they were good for sneezing, when of course they are only good for nettle stings.

Then the King tripped over the Prime Minister's foot and landed head first into a simply enormous pile of Christmas cards his several aunts had been sending him for years and years and which the Queen had only just been able to bring herself to throw away.

They searched and searched amongst the waste paper. They burrowed amongst old bills. They enveloped themselves in torn envelopes. They crawled about on old catalogues. They kept on finding each other but nothing else of any importance until they were tired out. And still no treaty found and the Imperial Conference due for the next day! The King could almost hear the wars beginning and the thrones falling and the price of food beginning to go up.

'Ha!' the King said, standing up suddenly and tipping the Prime Minister head over heels into several rolls of discarded wallpaper. 'Thinking about the price of food reminds me that I have got some sandwiches. Let's eat them and have a rest before we proceed with the search.'

'Yes, please,' said the Prime Minister who came stamping out of the rubbish heap with a roll of different-coloured wallpaper stuck on each leg like a pair of unreasonable sort of· top-boots.

So they sat down on a nice grassy bank while the King took out his sandwiches and undid the package.

'Cod-liver oil and turnip-tops!' he yelled.

'What?' cried the Prime Minister, thinking he meant that was what was in the sandwiches. 'No, not for me, thank you. I'll have a banana.'

'Don't talk to me, don't talk to me,' cried the King, getting up and starting to wave his hands in the air. 'Hooray! Hooray!'

He danced across and right through the middle of the rubbish heap, kicking up waste paper in all directions and starting the guards off sneezing again.

'Look at this, look at this,' he screamed, waving something in his hand. He waved it so quickly that the Prime Minister couldn't look at it.

'Look!' he cried, stopping waving. 'It's the secret treaty.'

And so it was. The Queen had found the secret treaty in the waste-paper basket, and not knowing what it was, but finding it was a nice crackly sort of piece of paper that might be useful for wrapping things up in she had kept it and she had actually wrapped the King's sandwiches in the very secret treaty he had gone out to look for.

So everything was all right. There were no wars. Thrones stopped where they were. The price of food went down instead of up. The end of it all was that the Swali of Swallowbitz took care of the secret treaty, but you can see how awful it is when you get all mixed up with secret treaties which mustn't be spoken about to anybody.

CLASSICS TO TREASURE

From Random House Children's Publishers

Also available to collect:

The Story of Doctor Dolittle

HUGH LOFTING

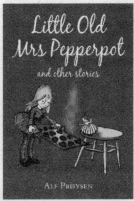

Little Old Mrs Pepperpot and other stories

ALF PRØYSEN

Emil and the Detectives

ERICH KÄSTNER

The Silver Sword

IAN SERRAILLIER

The Wolves of Willoughby Chase

JOAN AIKEN

The incredible adventures of Professor Branestawm

NORMAN HUNTER

CLASSICS TO TREASURE

From Random House Children's Publishers

Welcome to the wonderfully nutty, fabulously entertaining mishaps of Professor Branestawm!

Professor Branestawm is madly sane and cleverly dotty. He simply hasn't got the time to think about ordinary things - his head is too full of brilliant ideas and wild inventions. Yet the professor's absent-mindedness means that his devices rarely seem to work as they should, and wacky mishaps are never far behind . . .

These ingenious stories have delighted generations of children, and are as timelessly hilarious today as they ever were.

CLASSICS TO TREASURE

From Random House Children's Publishers

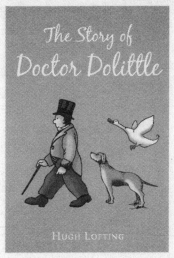

Once upon a time, many years ago – when our grandfathers were little children – there was a doctor, and his name was Dolittle – John Dolittle M.D.

Doctor Dolittle likes animals. In fact, he likes them so much he fills his house with every kind of creature imaginable and even learns to talk their language. And when the Doctor hears of a terrible sickness among the monkeys in Africa, soon he and his animal friends are setting off on the most unforgettable adventure . . .

These classic stories of the most extraordinary animal doctor there ever was continue to delight and captivate generation after generation.

CLASSICS TO TREASURE

From Random House Children's Publishers

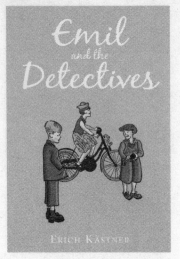

If Mrs Ticshbein had known the adventures her son Emil would have in Berlin, she'd never have let him go. But after meeting a mysterious man on the train, Emil falls fast asleep and awakens to discover that both the man, and the seven pounds his mother gave him, have gone missing.

Emil is determined to get it back – and when he teams up with the detectives he meets in Berlin, it's just the start of a marvellous money-retrieving adventure . . .

A classic and influential story, *Emil and the Detectives* remains an enthralling read.